A Tale of Dreams and Demons

Liz Hernandez

Dedication

I dedicate this book to my little sister, my biggest fan and best supporter. May you never lose the spark of creativity and love of art. And for all those weirdos who like something a little too much.

Prologue

Everything is a lie. Stories. Movies. They sell you on their tales and wonder, but in the end it's nothing. Happy endings aren't given to the weak and powerless.

Melosia thought these bitter words over and over cursing her existence and fate. She gazed at the dim white walls of the infirmary barely lit by the flickering candles that lined the walls. Wrapping her bandaged arms tight around herself she squeezed as another wave of sickness, pain, and despair washed over her with the vastness of the seas.

Fresh tears sprang to her eyes as she whimpered softly. Honestly she was shocked she still had tears and that she could make any kind of noise after the shrieking tantrum she had thrown.

What had gone wrong? What had she ever done to deserve this? Just when everything in her life finally felt like it had meaning and purpose it was snatched away with realities ice cold grip. The happiness she had thought she found came crashing down like heavy rain, just like that day. That day that started it all. She gritted her teeth at the thought of how stupid she had been romanticizing fiction and fantasy.

Reaching to the small wooden side table the girl's fingers ghosted over the cold metal of a butter knife. She gingerly lifted it up twirling it in her fingers. The candle light flashed eerily in its blade. She released a bitter bark of laughter looking at her pathetic visage in the knife at her empty dark eyes that stared back hollowly at her.

"Why did it turn out this way?" She croaked, voice barely audible even over the crackling of the torches. How she wished she could go back and live a boring life. If only she hadn't said yes and never agreed to stay. If only she hadn't craved adventure instead of the normal humdrum of high school. If only.

Chapter 1

- -

Melosia stared into the crackling flames of the fire as her sister roasted a marshmallow. An owl hooted in the crisp night air.

"Alma, you know what it means when an owl hoots three times?"

The young girl looked up, face paling and eyes going wide, the irritation she had fostered most of the day replaced with fear.

Mel paused letting her sister stew in thought. She crept forward with claw-like hands. "Darkness...death."

"La Lechuza," Alma whispered, turning to stare into the dark woods.

"Or," Mel paused to poke her sister, "if we go with the logic of Knights of the Night you're cursed to become an owl in three days."

With that last statement the frown returned to Alma's small face. With a huff she shook her wavy dark locks with a jerk of her head looking away from Mel. "Thanks for reminding me that instead of watching the season finale marathon we are camping."

"Come on, you love the family camping spot."

"Not this weekend I don't and we haven't come down here in like five years does it even count anymore."

"We'll watch the episodes when we get back alright."

"Sure we will. You'll just push it to the side and forget until there are too many to watch and quit the show, just like you do with the school clubs every year."

"I don't quit that often," Mel said, placing a hand over her chest aghast.

Her younger sister stared up at her with knowing eyes. "What about book club this year?"

"I didn't like what we were reading, it was boring. That's all," Mel stammered trying to come up with a decent excuse.

Alma crossed her arms appearing like a miniature version of their mother and made a tsk noise. "That's not what mom said."

"It doesn't matter if I change my hobbies or classes just because I don't like them or if it's boring. I'm doing what she wants anyway," she said more to herself than her sister.

A sharp whistle put an end to the conversation as their mother, Minerva, called for them from the open door of the cabin. Her outline is a dark shape to the bright light leaking around her.

Alma hummed, skipping into the cabin leaving Mel alone with the fire and her thoughts. Huffing she lifted the heavy pale of water and poured it on the fire with a hiss as gray smoke bellowed up obscuring the bright stars that lit the night.

Mel walked toward the old wooden cabin. Alma was right they hadn't been back in a long time, but Mel still remembered all the trails like it was yesterday. Walking across the creaking floorboards toward her room she felt a lump in her throat. The last time they were here was to spread their father's ashes.

The memories of that day came flooding back. How she'd run off to hide in the woods. The feelings of sadness smothered her insides and made it hard for her to breathe so she ran until she tripped and got a splinter. She curled up on the forest floor to cry because her father was always the one who removed splinters for her, and with him gone, who would do it. Who would protect her? Who would play the villain when her and Alma played pretend?

Then her uncle Lupus appeared and brought her back. He fixed the splinter and told her stories of his adventures to cheer her up. He even said that she could come with him one of these days. She'd liked that idea, but it didn't last long.

Once they had returned Lupus and her mother spoke in harsh whispers while her father's family talked in loud Spanish. The rest of the memory was a blur. She remembered her finger bleeding and the sound of her mother's hand across her uncle's face. And the argument that followed. That night she had lost not only her father but her uncle as well in a sense because he never visited again.

Mel sighed. She had waited for uncle Lupus to come back over the years wishing that he would fulfill that promise for adventure. Yet the years went by and she got older and more accustomed to a life of boredom than one of wonder. She wished for more than anything that fantasy was real and that one day she would go on a real adventure like in the shows she watched with Alma. *But those are the dreams of a kid,* she thought as she walked to the old window that always opened on its own from age, to close and lock it along with the memories.

Chapter 2

"En garde!" Mel yelled clashing with Alma in front of the cabin, the browning grass crunching under foot.

The two were in a heated sword fight with all the grace of a child swatting at flies. They argued about what characters they would be from Knights of the Night, as their mother watched with light amusement at their childish antics.

"I'm older, so I should be the main character by birth rite. Meaning, I will win this fight because the main character always wins."

"No, if we go by age you should be the villain, because he's older than James, meaning I would win."

"Don't 'well actually' me, pipsqueak!"

"I didn't say that! And you're only a little bigger than me."

"Do the brave warriors want to stop for sandwiches or shall I feed them to the birds?" Minerva called, smirking as they threw down the sticks and raced toward her.

Mel got there first, grabbed the small wicker basket from Minerva's hands, and pranced backwards to keep it out of Alma's reach as she trailed behind. Mel kept it up for a little bit longer before plopping down in front of a large tree some distance from the cabin. She spread a yellow tarp and sat down, then handed her pouting sister a sandwich. Looking up as she ate, she saw a vulture circling the sky above them.

"Did you finish your homework?" Alma asked.

"Did you?"

"No, but don't you have to finish that list to graduate?"

"No, it's just to help pick out what classes I'll take for the next few years. I'll have Mom put down whatever she wants," Mel said, leaning back.

"But shouldn't you answer truthfully?"

Mel turned to look at her sister then turned her attention back to the vulture. Silence crept on as she thought. Her eyes roamed to the sun and transparent moon. "What's the point? Dreams are like stars. No matter how long you gaze at them, they will always be far out of reach."

Alma stared at her blinking slowly. "Just become an astronaut; then anything is possible."

The matter of fact way she said it had Mel laughing. "I guess that would solve the problem. So you think no matter the cost, just go for it."

"Yup. Being an astronaut would be cool. I could meet an alien," she said, dreamily.

"That would be cool, but you know what would be cooler?" Mel paused, leaning over. "Being a knight, traveling the lands, and punching a dragon."

Alma giggled, nodding in agreement. "Where are you going?" She asked as Mel started walking away.

"I'm going on a bike ride."

"I wanna come too."

"Catch me, if you can," Mel said, racing back toward the cabin.

"Wait up!"

"Never!!"

The tires of the bicycle squeaked as she pushed it toward the bike path and her sister's calls to slow down.

"Melosia, be careful there could be bears and for the love of," Minerva called out, stamping her foot. "Wait for your sister!"

"What! Can't hear you?" Mel replied, as she jumped onto the silver bike and pushed off down the woodland trail.

"Adios, loser!" She added as she waved behind at Alma who struggled after her.

Mel glided down the road, her mind drifting off, imagining what it would be like to travel and explore. Not outer space; she'd settle for earth. What a life that would be; to just go where the winds take her and to have an adventure that would make any nerd jealous. She was so caught up in her thoughts, she almost didn't catch the flash of red that dashed out before her. She slammed on her breaks and jerked the handles. But she veered off the road, skidded on a puddle, and flipped off the bike, and onto the hard leafy earth.

Dazed, Mel stared at the fox that cocked its head quizzically then darted off. She blinked and looked around her surroundings. The sky was darkening. The musky, stale stench of earth filled her head. A few crows stared down at her, hopping from branch to branch. *Go away, I'm not dead,* she thought, her head ringing from being jostled in the helmet. Grimacing, she rolled onto her feet. Her back stung. Taking one step caused pain to shoot through her leg. She winced, realizing that her pants felt sticky at the knee. Releasing a shaky breath, she looked down.

Blood dripped out of a gash on Mel's knee, staining her torn jeans. She brought her fist to her mouth, attempting to keep from gagging or screaming. She stumbled to her bike. *I need to get back to the cabin or I might die out here*, she thought with a small pained chuckle.

Using the bicycle as a crutch, Mel hobbled forward, leaving a wobbly trail of blood. Chewing on her lip helped with the pain as she shuffled. It felt like she was getting nowhere at this rate but there was no way she could ride her bike like this. The image of blood gushing from her knee while pedaling made her gag.

A low grumble trilled through the air. Mel turned and her mouth went dry. Her vision tunneled. All she could see was the large brown bear. It was maybe twenty feet away, sniffing around. It started lapping something off the ground. The world teetered when she realized it was licking her blood. She glared accusingly at her knee feeling betrayed by her own body. Blaming her knee was stupid, but if she got eaten by a bear, she had to blame something.

Luckily the beast hadn't noticed her yet. Grinding her teeth, Mel tentatively lifted her leg to get on the bike seat, keeping her eyes locked on the bear.

"Mel! Sis, there you are!" A small voice called out, causing Mel's knees to jerk.

Up ahead on the path, Alma was riding toward her with a giddy grin proud to have finally caught up. It was obvious that she had not noticed the bear. She hopped off the bike and walked toward Mel.

Pain shot through her knee as Mel lunged at her sister, slamming a clammy hand over Alma's mouth. "Don't make a sound. Look," Mel hissed, turning her head back toward the bear.

The color drained from Alma's face as she gave a shaky nod.

"Start pushing your bike and be quiet," Mel said. As they both moved forward, Mel felt nauseous. The loud drumming in her ears and the squeaks of the bike tires rang like explosions in the stillness.

Snap.

The sound of the branch cracking under Mel's foot was like thunder. Looking back, her dark eyes met with the bear's. Licking its chops, it stared at Mel and Alma. Then, it bared its teeth in some semblance of a smile, causing Mel's stomach to twist violently. Her sister clamped her hands over her mouth as terror gripped them both. Tears began to flow from both their eyes as the bear stood on its hind legs.

Chapter 3

Mel had seen bears at the zoo. She knew they could be large, but the size of this bear was unnatural. It had to be over ten feet tall. Her mouth opened, but all that came out was a pathetic squeak as her throat spasmed. Would she die out here with Alma, never to be found? Or would their grizzly remains be discovered? *Now is not the time for stupid puns! We have to get away,* she thought, shaking her head and pushing Alma.

"Ride! Don't stop or look back!" She yelled, jumping on her bike. The bear roared behind them as she pushed through her pain, fueled by fear.

She pedaled like hell as rain began to drizzle down in chilly splashes. *No, no, no, no,* she chanted internally as the path became slippery and the bear gained on them. Any minute it would get her and after that it'd get Alma. Tears blurred her vision as she prayed to be rescued.

Alma's bike teetered, and she tumbled onto the road. Mel was going too fast to break. As she passed Alma, Mel saw her small face was ashen with fear. Mel flung herself off her bike, pain shooting through her wrists as she landed on the forest floor.

The bear was feet from Alma, stalking slowly toward her.

Terrible images flashed through Mel's mind. Her fingers curled around the rough surface of a rock. She flung it with all her might and hit the bear in the head. It stopped, stared at her, then turned back to her sister.

Rising to her feet, Mel threw another rock. "Hey! Get away from my sister! Hey!"

The bear turned toward Mel and rose to its full height with a roar while she yelled back.

"Alma, get out of here!" She yelled, locking eyes with the bear.

"Bu-bu-"

"GO!"

Alma pulled her bike up, tears and rain plastering her hair to her face. The bear turned after her but Mel hit it with another rock.

"OVER HERE!" Mel yelled, jumping back onto her bike leading the bear away.

Her heart hurt and her head was spinning. She had to get this monster away from her sister even if it meant sacrificing herself. Her knee's burned as she pushed on, the bear gaining on her with every bound.

A root sticking out of the ground caught the tires, and Mel crashed on the side of the road. Rolling to her stomach, digging her nails into the ground, she attempted to crawl away but a large claw slammed onto her back pushing her down. Mud filled her mouth and nose.

Mel said another prayer for someone to save her, a hunter or a passing car, anything. She didn't want to die like this; weak and alone. If anything, she needed to let Alma get away. She wiggled in vain. The claws cut into her, the pain burned making her thrash. She tried to yell but nothing came out. It was over. Her life, cut short. She closed her eyes, going limp praying that Alma made it to safety.

The rain intensified. As she was blasted with the downpour, she heard a thump. She waited for the hot breath and sting of fangs but nothing happened as the weight on her back was released followed by a heavy impact that rattled her. Cracking open an eye, she screamed at the bear's headless corpse, its blood seeped into the earth. Rising to her knees, she brought a shaky hand to her mouth only to see it coated in blood. Bile rose up as she realized she was covered in its hot blood. She retched violently onto the ground.

A gentle hand patted her head. Relieved, she gazed up to see the face of her savior, only to find that her hero was...Estranged family? Her uncle stood before her, his dark hair flat from the drizzling rain. His brown eyes that were usually filled with mirth were creased with concern.

"Uncle Lupus, what-?" She paused, waving at the bear's corpse. "How?"

Shaking his head, he reached into his traveling cloak, and with an audible rip tore a piece of his dark shirt off. "Don't worry about that right now. Let's wrap that knee."

He wrapped Mel's knee with the soft fabric, then looked at her back. "Your back isn't bad, barely bleeding, it can wait. Climb on up, time to get you back to Minerva," he said, squatting down with a grimace. "Oh, Minerva is going to blame me for this."

Mel winced, climbing onto his back. "What makes you think that?"

"Have you met your mother?" He winked, picking up her bike to wheel it back.

Mel turned to take one last glance at the bear, then rubbed her eyes in confusion. It almost appeared that vines had started to grow around the bear. Shaking her head, she chalked it up to light-headedness from blood loss.

The rain splattered onto the leaves in heavy drops around them. Mel blinked her eyes, feeling heavy. "Are you going to explain why you suddenly appeared and killed a bear or will I just have to leave that explanation up to my own imagination?"

His back tensed then shook softly from his laugh. "I guess I have no choice. I was coming to see you to tell you happy birthday. The big one-six, right?"

"You're a few days late and a whole year early all at the same time, Uncle. Impressive. It's my fifteenth birthday."

He paused to look back at her, his eyes scrunched up in thought before walking again. "Fifteen is still a big age. Right on the cusp of adulthood. When I was that age I had already started my travels. My, how the time flies by."

Mel let out a clipped laugh. "I remember when you told me you'd take me on an adventure once."

"I did. The option is still there if you want," he hummed.

"What?!" Mel jerked, throwing the fatigue away now alert.

"Yes, how can I not spend more time with my favorite niece," he said. "But the problem is that Minerva would never allow you to leave. You see, that's why she got so angry at me last time."

Mel leaned closer to her uncle's face. "I always wondered what the argument was about. Mom would get mad when I asked and just say we were better off without you."

Lupus cringed. "Man, that's mean."

They continued to walk in silence as Mel stared out into the dark forest as the rain poured around. After some more time passed it became relevant that her uncle was not going to continue unless prompted. She shrugged. "Uncle, why did you leave? What did you say?"

"All I said was that it might be easier for her to raise just Alma and that I would take you in. Since I see a bit of myself in you I thought it would be a good idea. Minerva took it all out of proportion though. She went as far as forbidding me from seeing you all ever again. I thought that now was a good time to try again. The blood in our family is special Melosia and I can tell that you are destined for greatness."

"Well, good luck with that. Mom will never agree."

"When it comes down to it Melosia," he paused to look at her, "it's your life and some choices need to be made with your own heart even if it goes against the will of others."

The cabin's silhouette appeared against the setting sun as the rain stopped. A light mist and fog had settled low to the sodden ground. As they got closer, the door flung open and Minerva ran toward them. She dragged them into the house talking incoherently. She ignored Lupus while she tended her daughter's back.

Once Mel was seated onto the couch with an ice pack on her, the chill began creeping into her back dulling the pain. She watched with held breath as Minerva turned to Lupus with a snarl.

"What the hell! Why are you here? Why is Melosia hurt and covered in blood? And what is the nonsense Alma is saying!"

"It's alright, Mom, most of the blood belonged to the bear," Mel said, having a hard time breathing as her sister flung herself on her squeaking. Mel released a squeak of discomfort as her back stung red with pain.

"Bear...What bear?!"

"The one that tried to eat us, Uncle decapitated it, and still hasn't explained how," Mel replied, snatching up a coarse white towel her sister had brought to rub at her face staining it burgundy. She wrinkled her nose at the sight.

"With a sword," he said, examining his nails.

"Cool!" The sisters yelled in unison, staring up at him in wonder.

Spinning on her heels Minerva pointed at Uncle Lupus. "This is your fault, isn't it?"

"I save my niece, and get accused. I can't win with you," He waved her off. "The attack was a coincidence. We should count our luck that I was coming to see Melosia."

"Nothing is ever a coincidence with you and I thought I made myself clear that you are never allowed near my girls again."

"Minerva, please."

"No, you tried to use my grief to make it easier to take one of my children," she stomped around the room with every word.

"She is one of us. The test should have been enough for you to open your eyes, but I think the recent events should prove it."

"I don't care. She is my child."

"It's her choice. At least let me explain it to her."

"No, I left that life behind with my father; and I left you behind at the funeral. If you had any love in your heart for us you wouldn't only appear when things are good for you! That place took my mother and gave my father unspeakable nightmares; I refuse to put my child through that," she spat every word at him.

Lupus clutched Minerva's shoulders, trapping her in place and forced her to look him in the face. "Minerva, listen to reason. If I wasn't here you wouldn't have daughters to even see anymore. Which is why I tested them back then; to make sure they would be safe and Mel is not safe here. Not anymore. I'm doing this out of love."

"Then how come in fifteen years nothing like this has ever happened before? We're safe here," Minerva leaned her head into her brother's chest, the fight leaving her, like the barely audible whispers of her words.

"You don't have to worry, I'll keep her safe. What else is family for?" He replied with a tender look upon his face as Minerva wiped her eyes.

Lupus released her from his grip and turned to Mel with a small smile.

"Listen to me carefully, Melosia. You and I are special, our heritage is different from that of your mother and sister, even though you are related by blood. Because of this difference demons, like that bear, are attracted to you. Are you willing to put your family, friends, anyone you love in danger by staying? You should never leave your's and others safety to chance. Come with me and I'll teach you how to defend yourself."

Mel stared at her uncle's outstretched hand, her eyes drifted to behind him where her mother and sister stood holding each other. Visions of carnage flashed through her mind. Her family, ripped apart by the bear, blood everywhere. The feeling of helplessness when the bear pinned her, the horror of waiting for her death. She never wanted to feel that again. She stared down at her trembling hands, the copper, splotchy stains still lingered refusing to be removed. How likely was this to happen again? Or was this all some sick prank? The thoughts and unease clogged her throat. She attempted multiple times to get the words out of her mouth.

"You're joking right? This is insane."

"Mi Amor, what he said is true. The first ten years of my life I lived there. It's a different place; sometimes I think back to that part of my life and just think it was a dream," Minerva said in almost a whisper. "Yet it wasn't. My mother was taken by that world and I've done everything I could to forget it."

Minerva stood straight turning on Lupus with a snarl slapping his hand away. "And that is why you will leave and you will never come back! I don't care about family ties not anymore. You stay away from Melosia, that test is a lie, she is nothing like you!"

Mel lounged up in shock at her mother's tone. "Mom?!"

"No, Melosia, this is the end! Get. Out. Lupus." She seethed.

Lupus' face fell as he lifted his hands. "I see when I'm not wanted. I'm glad I atleast got to see you kids again."

He walked to the door head down cast and left into the rainy night.

Minerva turned to her daughters after slamming and locking the door. "Go to bed. We leave in the morning."

"But-"

"No Melosia, we leave in the morning."

Mel clutched her hands fighting back tears of conflicting emotions. The horrors of the day and what could have happened lay twisted in her head. She ran to her room throwing herself onto her bed to cry in private the tears of fear and shame, the shame that she wanted to go but evidently that choice wasn't even hers to make.

As Mel sat on the bed utterly exhausted and confused she fidgeted with the bandage on her knee. She sighed going over to the room's window to close it again as the old hinges lifted up once more,letting the night breeze in. She noticed something small and white in the corner of the window. She picked up the small piece of paper and read the small message. She crushed the note, her heart spasming with guilt at what she was planning on doing.

Mel was in the process of shoving the last of her things into her bag when her door squeaked open causing her to jerk knowing she was caught. Turning she saw Alma standing blurry eyed in the doorway.

"What are you doing?"

"Packing early so we can leave tomorrow like mom said. What's up?"

"I'm scared, can I sleep in here?"

Mel cursed inwardly and put on a small smile. "Of course lay down. I probably won't go to sleep for a while because I'm going to read. Noche my little buddy"

Sitting on the corner of the old bed Mel feigned reading until she was sure her sister was asleep. She began to stand up when the door opened again. Mel's stomach twisted as her mom walked in looking them over.

"I'm sorry we have to leave early but it's for the best. I'll make it up to you, mi corazon," she whispered, placing a hand on Mel's head.

"I know mom," Mel replied, tingling from head to foot with nerves.

"I know you had a scary day but try to go to sleep. Love you."

"Love you too mom."

Mel waited until she heard her mom's door closed and then with a sense of guilt and excitement gently pushed the old window open feeling the night air rush in past her. She pulled her backpack on and crawled through the window disappearing into the night for the adventure she longed for at the cost of leaving her stars behind.

Mel trudged through the mud and puddles down the dark walking path led by the light of the full moon. The sounds of owls and the dripping of water onto the sodden ground echoed in her head. Her thoughts were jumbled yet she knew what she was doing. Like the note said she was following her heart and it led to adventure.

A figure morphed from the shadows making Mel jump and slam her hand painfully over her mouth to stifle her yell. She cursed inwardly thinking her mom saw through her only to see it was her uncle. She exhaled through her nose loudly. "You almost gave me a heart attack."

"My bad."

"Where are we going and how are we getting there? I don't think even a year headstart will keep mom from catching up and grounding me for life."

"Then let's begin, Cornelia," he said, as another cloaked figure appeared from the gloom.

"Good evening," the cloaked woman said, with a small bow. Her voice held a melody like chimes and a forest. "Shall we begin."

The women pulled out a carved decorated staff and began to sway. She hummed, twirling the staff as the bells cut through the chilly air. Chanting low, she danced in a fast temp, her feet prancing through the damp and cold grass. The air seemed to hum and the wind picked up. The clouds in the sky began to fly by, covering and uncovering the moon and stars. Power hung in the air along with the sound of bells, wind, and chanting. She slammed the staff abruptly into the ground, ivy and ferns unfurled at the place of impact and darkness descended upon them.

Mel's center of gravity shook and her stomach lurched as the world began to dissolve. Her ears buzzed and tears crept into her eyes, her heart hammered in her chest. The figures of trees wavered and blurred making her think of her mother and sister she was leaving. It was almost like a canvas being stripped for a new painting to unravel. She casted her eyes to the sky as her mind spun. The stars and moon gleamed weakly, dissolving away. She stared back at her family cabin in the distance, thinking how she was leaving the true stars of her life.

Chapter 4

M el felt suffocated by the never ending darkness that crushed her from all around. Images of her life flashed rapidly before her eyes. Birthdays, a funeral, friends, a fox, and her family. The pictures merged, blurring together like a jumbled film reel. Her lungs burned and her throat felt raw. Was she dying? Dark colors slowly dripped into her vision, revealing a large curved staircase that led up to three different floors. Her shaking knees collapsed, crashing onto a cold stone floor. She barely registered the pain in her injured knee as waves of vertigo overtook her, causing her head to spin.

"Wh-what the actual hell was that?!" She choked out, glaring accusingly at her uncle. Grimacing, she placed a hand to her mouth to try and stave off the bile that seemed to rise up.

"Oh, I must have forgotten to mention that we were jumping dimensions. The first trip can be a little difficult," he casually stated, eyes twinkling clearly amused by her reaction. Giving her a sheepish grin, he rubbed the back of his head. "Sorry about that."

"You forgot to mention. That seems like a very important detail to forget. Oh, we aren't going down the street or to another state, no; we are going to another world!"

"If you knew, would it have changed anything?" He asked with a slight smirk. Mel silently puffed her cheeks out, turning away in silence. "See, wouldn't have made a difference. If I did mention it you would have assumed I was crazy." He added with a bark of laughter.

Mel crossed her arms, petulantly giving him the silent treatment much to his amusement. He leaned down to pat her on the back but she leaped up, flinching at the twinge of pain that bolted through her back and knees. Wobbling, she backed away from him, glaring at him and inching closer to Cornelia. The woman stepped in front of her, shielding her from Lupus' bemused looks.

"If you are done, I will be taking my leave. It was a pleasure to meet you, Melosia," Cornelia said, pulling down her dark hood, revealing long wavy locks of snow white hair that framed her dark face and vivid green eyes. She was intimidatingly beautiful, making it hard for Mel to reply. "Lupus, stop teasing the poor child. Shame, for not warning her." She added, placing a hand on her shoulder before ascending the curved stairs to the third floor.

"Fine, fine. Follow me to your room unless you fancy the idea of sulking and having to sleep on the cold floor for the night," he walked down the left corridor, calling over his shoulders as the torch's flames danced.

Mel remained standing and looked up at the tall domed ceiling where a large gilded, candle chandelier hung, giving off only a faint light. She bit her lip as the room appeared to grow darker and the eerie silence closed in around her. She turned on her heel and ran after her uncle's receding footsteps, not wanting to be alone in a strange unfamiliar place.

Mel followed Lupus down the long hallway, the only light coming from the warm glow of the torches. They passed rows of doors that lined both sides of the walls and every few doors, a tapestry would decorate the wall. The tapestries depicted people fighting large animals, each outlined with bright red and gold borders showing running dogs. She ran a finger over the thick material, the threads bumping against her fingertips while her mind wandered. The sound of clinking metal brought her attention back to reality. Her uncle had stopped at a door just a few feet away, rifling through a ring of silver keys.

Pulling out a key with a wooden handle, Lupus unlocked the door with a slight click. The door creaked open and stale air rushed out. The small bow and flourish he made with his hand caused the girl to want to roll her eyes.

Candles flared to life as if lit with magic as the duo walked in, illuminating the small empty room. All that was present was a canopy bed and a wooden dresser. A door on the side of the wall was cracked open showing tiles. A small end table was beside the bed along with an empty bookshelf. There was nothing that personalized the room; it was a blank slate.

"It's not much, but it's yours for now. You'll be able to do what you like with it, and it has everything you might need; a bed, a dresser, and a bathroom," Lupus slid a hand over the carved door of the dresser, its ivy pattern was intricate.

"That's if I stay at all, but thanks. I like it," she said, sitting on the plush bed and inspecting the matching carved patterns of ivy in the poles.

"I have a hard time believing you won't stay. Minerva never liked it here, but I can tell you will. Tomorrow you can explore to your little heart's content. The mess hall is under the grand staircase on the first floor, the one you saw when we arrived. On the third floor you can only go into the library; nowhere else is interesting up there. Feel free to go anywhere you want, just don't leave the village. I'm sure you will love this place as I do. Good night," he said kindly, turning and leaving her alone.

Unpacking her bag didn't take anywhere as long as Mel would have expected, since it wasn't much to begin with. She laid the framed photo and book, a companion edition of *Knights of the Night*, on the nightstand, and hung her clothes up in the closet. After changing in the small tiled bathroom, she lay on her new bed, staring up at the ceiling, wondering if she just jumped at the first opportunity to just go on an adventure, to run away from her problems. She knew the truth of it; she was running away from the expected, trading it in for the unexpected.She was tired of the normal life and used fantasy as an escape for excitement. Her eyes grew heavy, her long lashes fluttering like dark butterflies.

"Also if you need anything just ask-"

"AHHH!" Mel shrieked. She had only closed her eyes for a second and her uncle seemed to materialize out of thin air. She clutched her chest, shooting daggers at him with her eyes.

"Sorry, I just thought I would pop in to see if you were all set up. Seems you are. Put that pillow down. It wouldn't do much damage, getting hit by something so soft and fluffy," he said jokingly.

"How about a book?" She replied lifting the thick book, it had survived both her's and Alma's bags multiple times and it would survive her uncle's face.

"That would do significantly more damage to my ruggedly handsome face. I think I'll leave you be, for now," he said, shutting the door.

Mel placed the book gently back on the end table and rolled onto her side to calm her breathing. She snickered a little, starting to feel excitement for the new world she would soon be part of. Even though her uncle might be crazy, that just might make the experience all the more fun. She bundled herself in the sheets, her irritation and fear from earlier completely gone replaced by wonder and excitement. Her life was taking an unexpected turn but she wasn't complaining.

Chapter 5

Opening her eyes Mel was confused to be in an unfamiliar place. Then she remembered that somehow she was now in another world, something she could only dream about previously. She'd just had a dream the images were fading from her memory but she remembered a black fox and a park. She yawned, stretching her arms wide, feeling waves of anticipation and jitters wash over her that almost surpassed the stinging from her back and knee. Smiling, she jumped out of bed then winced in instant regret, she gingerly dressed to start the first day of her new life, and hopefully the start of an amazing adventure.

She practically skipped down the corridor to the entrance with the staircase excitement overtaking her dull pains. Her shoes tapped on the stone floor. *This place has a real medieval feel to it,* she thought. At the top of the staircase, she took a moment to observe her surroundings in the large room since she hadn't the night before. The staircase was split on the first floor into two, leading to the second floor, and then curled to the third floor. The steps were wood, painted white and brown which matched the brown of the shining railings. In-between the staircase, just as Lupus had said, two large doors with gold handles stood with a sign reading "MESS HALL",that hung overhead. The clanking of heels on stone echoed off the walls of the right corridor. She turned only to get plowed down by an unseen assailant. All she caught was a blur of silver and blue. She landed painfully on her butt, causing her to grimace.

"I'm sorry about that. My wife can be like that sometimes, she's always rushing headlong into everything," a man with curly brown hair said. He reached a hand out for Mel which she took thankfully.

"I apologize again on her behalf. Tsume, wait for me," he said, again turning and running out the large double doors of the entrance, Mel assumed, as she caught a glimpse of a clear blue and pink morning sky before they closed again.

For a few seconds after she dusted herself off, Mel debated going straight through those dark doors gilded in gold to the unknown outside world. But willingly forgoing a meal was not in her character. She walked to the mess hall doors and grasped the handle, it's cold metal smooth under her palm. Taking a deep breath, she pulled it open.

A large mess hall greeted Mel; three long rows of tables that were oddly empty with only a few groups sitting sparsely about. She walked in slowly looking around and then took an empty chair. Breakfast meats, bread, soup, salads, and juices were laid across each table. She piled a variety of foods onto a plate, and tasted everything. A blissful grin bloomed across her face at how tasty everything was.

"I'm glad you like it. You must be the niece."

"What?" Mel mumbled, chewing a piece of bread. "Hey," she added, quickly noticing the man who was talking to her.

"Hey, indeed. The name is Oliver, I'm the head chef here," he introduced himself with a small bow, looking her over with his hazel eyes.

"I'm Melosia, but you can call me Mel, everyone normally does, less of a mouthful. Your cooking is excellent. First class," she replied, picking up another biscuit.

Oliver pulled out the seat across from her. He tossed his light tawny hair to the side, leaning across the table. She leaned away, making him smile.

"No need to be shy. Just trying to find old man Lupus in you, and I wanted to introduce myself. Anyway, if you ever need me, I'll be here. I can bet you'll get into some form of trouble if you're anything like your uncle, and by the way you eat, I can see that is true," he said, standing up and headed back to the kitchen.

After that, no one seemed that interested in her, but Mel could have sworn she felt a few pairs of eyes on her while she finished eating. Getting up, she decided to check out her new home before exploring the outside village.

First, she went down the left corridor where her room was. Most of the rooms she could look through were empty and had cobwebs clinging to the beds. The doors would make a weird groan, as if they were vacuum-sealed. Other doors she came across were locked, and some rooms had old weapons in them, rusted and broken. At the end of the hall she found an infirmary of clean, empty white beds lining the white walls. The room hurt her eyes a bit with how dark everything else had been. She saw two small children dart into another room as a woman came walking towards her, she was pale with a silver bob. Her golden eyes shone warmly, making her look almost angelic.

"Good morning, dear, are you injured?"

"No, not really that badly," she replied, staring in the direction the children ran.

"Don't mind them, they are a bit shy around new faces. You must be Melosia, then. Lupus has told me about you. My name is Storm. If it's not too much let me examine your back injuries. Lupus told me it wasn't bad, but I cannot overlook an injury."

Mel headed back down the hallway resisting the urge to scratch at the bandages that itched on her back or the slight smell lingering from the herbal cream Storm had put on them. She walked fast in an attempt to escape the smell of herbs that stung her nose. She was glad Storm hadn't noticed her knee injury just thinking about more of the herbal smells made her light headed.

The right side corridor was much the same as the left; doors, tapestries, and more doors. Some rooms were open, some closed. Some had odds and ends and others had nothing. At the end of the hall, Mel came into an empty dark room with only a red and black chair in the back. She touched the plush velvet of the chair and gazed up at the wall behind it. A symbol was painted in red of a crescent moon with a star. It was a lovely design that reminded her of a necklace she bought Alma once. There wasn't much to look at in this room so she headed back to the main entrance, staring back at the symbol one more time.

Mel walked up the grand staircase, sliding her hand over the polished wooden railing that was smooth and cold from much use. Going down the left, she found a small sitting room, at the end, with a large bay window, looking out into the village and distant mountains. Only a few people were sitting around in the room. They waved to her in greeting and she nodded back. Down the right hall she found a large room full to the brim with weapons of every kind. Swords, lances, axes, and bows lined the walls in racks. She inspected the weapons. Some were real, others made of wood; she imagined wielding them in various ways. Some men were sparing off to the side, and she watched them for a bit of time, fully enraptured by the way they moved. She felt like she could have watched forever but didn't want to waste too much of her day.

All Mel had left to find was the library on the third floor. She gazed up the stairs. Walking up, she wondered why she was only allowed to go to the library. If it was because there was nothing up there that's odd because there's a whole lot of nothing on the lower floors too. Could there be secrets that the third floor hid?

Compared to the other floors the third floor was much darker and colder. The darkness was almost palpable, sending chills where it clung. The torches' dancing flames barely lit the passageways. Mel walked down the dark left corridor, her steps echoed through the deserted area, bouncing off the walls. The hallway had barely any doors until she arrived at the end. The double doors at the end were glass with etched flowers accented in gold, and above them a frosted sign spelled out the word library in cursive swirls.

With a triumphed smile, Mel gently pushed the doors apart to enter the spacious room. It was like heaven. Books with vibrant colors were everywhere. Ceiling high bookshelves lined the walls along the two rows with soft red chairs. The simple comforting fragrance of paper, leather, and wood hung in the air making her feel at ease.

She spent what must have been hours browsing the aisles and reading the spines of the different books. Books of history, geography, legend, and more were in front of her. She chose a red bound leather book about the tales of a pirate crew and sat down to read for a small bit. The pages crinkled with each turn of the page.

Closing the door behind her, Mel stretched, cracking her stiff bones from sitting for almost two hours. Turning, she spotted a door she missed on her trek for the library. She glanced from side to side to make sure no one was watching as she turned the bronze stiff knob and slipped inside. She scrunched her nose at the stale, dusty air. The room was crowded with what seemed to be old junk covered in a thick dust. Swords, spears, and various items were piled around the musty room. But in the center of the small cluttered space was a sparkling glass case with a strange weapon placed upon a black stand. She walked up close, placing her hands on the cold glass that not a speck of dust resided on. The torches cast an eerie shadow across the curved black blade.

"What are you?" She asked, inspecting the odd weapon through the glass.

The weapon was a staff of polished black wood with a red leather grip in the middle. What was odd was the curved black blade with swirling silver ivy carved into its surface. The blade was parallel with the staff touching the end creating a crescent. At the end of the blade, a silver cap attached the blade to the staff. There appeared to be a peg with a decorative red cord with a pair of silver bells attached.

Mel marveled at the weapon, idea's flooding her mind about how it was meant to be used. A creak to her left jerked her back to reality. Glancing in the direction of the noise, she saw nothing. She was still alone, and somewhere she shouldn't be, she reminded herself. Briskly she left the room.

Back at the staircase, Mel stopped when a tingle made the hairs stand upon the back of her neck. The candles started to dim in and out, flickering and casting shadows that seemed to be moving on their own. She bit her bottom lip before curiosity won her over and she walked through the hall. The torches went out, leaving her in complete darkness. Then two flickered back on, highlighting a single door along the corridor. The torches all danced back to life as she reached for the knob, barely caressing it with her finger tips, her nerves on edge.

Pushing the door open, she stood before another empty room but the air was strange; cold and warm, feeling sticky with humidity. At the very back of the room stood a pair of round doors painted black with gold designs of the star and moon. The air was thick, making it hard to breathe. She took a tentative step forward. A hand placed itself on her shoulder, causing her to jump out of her skin in fright.

"What do you think you are doing?" A calm voice asked.

Mel spun on her heels to see a young man a couple years her senior standing behind her with his arms crossed. His purple hair was pulled up in a ponytail and his bangs covered his left eye. His right blue eye gazed at her judgmentally. A scowl marred his lovely face while he tapped his foot in impatience.

"Sorry. I was just having a look around,"she said after taking a deep breath to calm herself.

"If I was informed correctly, you are only allowed in the library and nowhere else on this floor," he stated calmly, looking her over. "Now you better get going or else I'll tell your uncle that you were snooping in places you shouldn't be. Here's an allowance from Lord Lupus as well," he added, tossing her a small leather pouch.

Mel's reaction was too slow and the pouch bounced on the floor with a small jingle as a few cold coins slipped out. She bent down scooping up the cold coins as the stranger watched with a look of judgment. Dusting herself off she started to retort back at him but he was walking away. He gave her a quick look over his shoulder with an icy blue eye. Understanding the unsaid message, she shuffled after him and then down the stairs to the first floor. She turned back and grimaced, not liking being scolded by a stranger and pulled the door open, getting blinded by the bright afternoon sun-light.

Mel used her arm to shield her eyes. Blinking, after a few minutes, her eyes adjusted, and she sucked in her breath. Before her was a large stair-case of carved stone that led down into a large village. From her bird's eye view, the village seemed to be in the shape of a circle with a small wall surrounding its edges. The roofs of all the buildings were red tinted and were in various sizes. She stared out in wonder at her new world. She hummed lightly as she hopped down the steps.

Mel stumbled off the last step huffing from how long the steps had been. Doubling over she took a few moments to reestablish herself. Turning on her heel she gazed up in wonder at the dark mansion that she had exited. Its dark walls appeared to sparkle in the afternoon light. Amazed by the beauty of the gothic style mansion, she didn't register the arrival of someone behind her. A gentle tap on the shoulder jolted her out of her stupor, making her jump again for the umpteenth time in one day.

"Sorry about that. It's beautiful, right?" A boy with gray silver hair asked, a warm and friendly smile gracing his face.

Chapter 6

"What?" Mel replied, staring at the stranger.

"The mansion," he pointed up. "It's beautiful."

She crossed her arms. "Do you want something?"

"No, I just saw you coming from the mansion. I'm going to go out on a limb and ask if you are old man Lupus' niece or grandchild? Something along those lines? It's what Johnathan told me when he was complaining about the old man's newest scheme," he said quickly, almost tripping over the words.

Mel nodded, somewhat dumb-founded. "I am, yes. Yes, I am. Lupus' niece, that's what I am."

"It's a pleasure. The name is Daniel. You could say I know your uncle quite well."

"I'm Melosia, but Mel for short. Should I be concerned that someone my age is friends with my uncle?" She joked, cocking her head to the side. "Is that why your hair is gray?"

"No worries there. If you want to be specific, I'm friends with a guy who works under him and if anyone would have gray hair from stress it would be Johnathan. My hair is natural," he blushed, laughing. "If you would like, I could give you a tour of Stella Luna."

"No thanks. No offense, but since it's my first day here I'd like to see everything myself."

"You could get lost."

"I get lost all the time. How hard could it be to find the dark mansion on a literal mountain of stairs."

"That's true, it's hard to miss."

"Glad you see my point," she said, walking away.

"I get it. How about I treat you to lunch, then we can maybe become friends? It's just I never knew Lupus had family and I'm curious," he smiled, trotting up next to her.

Mel stopped, turning on her heels. She wrinkled her nose in thought. Cons; stranger danger, talking to someone, and he could be dangerous. Pros; free food, knows Uncle, knows the town, and free food. She nodded, coming to the conclusion that the pros outweigh the cons and free food was in the mix. If life had taught her anything it was never to pass up a free meal. She jumped, pointing at him.

"I relent. But the first sign of anything weird and I'm liable to hit you with my shoe."

"There's a place right around the corner," he led her to a small building stopping abruptly and turned to her. "Why a shoe?"

"It's something my dad would warn us of when we'd be bad," she paused to drop her voice. "Listen to your mother or she'll get the chancla."

She covered her mouth to stifle her giggles at the bittersweet memory. "Chancla means shoe," she added, as they walked in.

The two sat and ordered a sandwich and began to chat. Daniel took the time to reintroduce himself and talk about inconsequential things. In Mel's opinion, it was a rather nice lunch and he had a very friendly demeanor, so she found his company relaxing. As they talked she noticed that the building was lit only by candles and the sun which gave it a warm dusty glow. Everything in the building was rustic and rough unlike the smooth slick look she was used to in the buildings from home. Once they finished eating, he led her out and began, as he so eloquently put it, "the grand tour," with an exaggerated bow.

The first stop on Daniel's tour led to a strip of land next to the mansion with a small white picket fence. Stone figure heads littered the land in neat rows. There was no need for him to even mention what she was looking at because she knew what it was, anyone would. A cold chill ran up her spine at the thought that a cemetery was so close to the place she would rest her head at night.

"Do you take all the girls you meet to the graveyard?" She joked as a crisp breeze blew by causing the grass to ripple like waves.

"No. Ironically, it's just the natural place to start a tour. It's in such an odd place, but for some reason the original founders of our lovely home thought it would be honorable to have the dead close by, not strange at all," he pointed in the next direction they would head off to and ushered her away from the solemn place.

Despite starting with a beacon of death, Daniel was a good tour guide. He seemed to know almost everything about the shops and stores that were scattered across the expanse. When they walked into some stores, Mel picked out a few odds and ends she wanted to add for decorations in her room; a few hanging paper lanterns that came in warm colors of red and gold. She paid using the gold coins, it was a straight forward currency. At one antique shop she stopped to stare into a small silver hand mirror with gilded lilies along the back. They reminded her of spring when she'd plant lilies with the family, they were always her mother's favorite. She sighed and put the mirror back, deciding that the lanterns and small paintings she had bought were enough on her budget, since she had no clue if her uncle would continue to give her an allowance.

Daniel brought her to another small field on the other side of the village with long browning grasses and a tall fence. He smiled at Mel and held up a finger, signaling her to wait a second, and then whistled. A sound of thumping filled the air as a group of horses ran to the edge of the fence. Mel jumped back with a squeal when a light tan mare tried to nuzzle her face.

"It's alright. They won't hurt you," Daniel laughed at the expression of discomfort on Mel's face. "See? She is a friendly girl," he patted the mare on the snout as she whinnied, shaking her dark mane.

"That's what you say. But you know how easy it is for an animal that big to kill and eat a small thing like myself. I'll take my chances over here, watching you play with the ponies," she replied, waving her hands in front of her face vigorously.

"A horse won't eat you. I can teach you the right handling methods if that would make you feel better. I thought we could go riding down the forest paths."

"It's more of the fact," she paused and licked her lips, not knowing whether she should tell him this; but he seemed so friendly and comforting. "My dad had promised to take me horseback riding, but he died before he could take me. And I never really did it because of that," she shrugged, frowning, feeling that heaviness that would never truly vanish from her chest.

"I'm sorry I didn't mean to trigger bad memories," he grimaced, sliding a hand through his bangs. "If you want, I could teach you to ride. That's if you want to learn and if the horse tries to eat you, you can hit me with the chacleta."

Mel snorted and covered her mouth. "It's chancla not chacleta."

She walked gingerly to the mare and touched the horse's velvet muzzle. "She doesn't look like she'd eat me, but the moment I fall out of the saddle I'm going to get you with the chancla."

Daniel smiled at her cheeky grin. Shrugging, he walked to one of the troughs that lined the fence pulling out some hay and split it with her to feed the horse.

"Does she have a name?"

"Sandy."

"Sandy? How plain. Was Thunderhoof taken?"

Daniel snorted and shook his head. "No, but I'll remember to have it put out there next time a horse needs to get named."

A playground came into view as they walked from the horses' field. Mel quickened her steps at the sight of the holy grail; unoccupied swings. With a bounce in her step, she plopped onto the leather seat, wrapping her fingers around the rusted, cold chains that held it up. Grinning, she kicked her legs back and forth as the metal creaked.

"It has been too long since I got to play on these," she said while Daniel watched leaning to the side.

He slid into the seat next to her. They swung in reverse; every time they crossed he would lean forward and grin. Mel's lips quirked up to reflect his own. His awkward charm was infectious. He made a funny face that caused her to snort.

A small group of children squealed and giggled in the background, running through the dirt. They chased each other up the slides and jumped onto the metal death trap known as a merry-go-round that would suck you under, though this one was wooden giving it an even more torturous look. It creaked as they attempted to push it and spin. Daniel jumped off the swing, grinning, and ran over to help them. Mel watched as he grabbed the faded wooden bars and ran, propelling the children around and around as they shrieked in excitement. Mel shrugged before jumping off the swing and joining them on it. She held on tight as he spun them, her hair whipping around her, the air trying to rip them all off.

The sun had barely begun its descent, painting the sky in a purple hue. Daniel slumped back into the swing, exhausted, as Mel tried to walk in a straight line, swaying a little. Her head was still spinning and her stomach twisted as she sat. She couldn't remember the last time she had this much carefree fun. Exhaling, Daniel tugged at the ends of his hair.

"Those kids are slave drivers."

"I should have got off sooner. Though it was quite entertaining when you tripped and face planted. Are you alright?"

"Don't laugh. My knees still sting, not to mention by bruised pride."

"Your knees will be fine. I smashed my knee escaping a bear like yesterday and I'm fine."

"What?!"

"Yeah, it was quite the grizzly situation."

The duo fell into fits of laughter before eventually falling silent. They sat swinging gently, watching as the sky changed color and the air got chillier, their breath coming out in little puffs. The sky was like a picture that was slowly being painted in watercolor. The reds, pinks, and purples blended into the dark blue that was starting to take hold. Small specs of white were beginning to pop up dotting the sky as the stars twinkled in and out.

"It's getting late. We should head back. Sorry we couldn't go through the whole village today, but I did show you all the most important parts," Daniel said, stretching his arms to the stars and leaning to the side.

"If we had rushed through it all, I don't think I would have had as much fun," Mel replied, jumping off and walking in what she thought was the right direction.

Daniel started laughing and pointed over her shoulder in the opposite direction. "Wrong way, and what was that earlier about not getting lost because of the giant mansion on a mountain of stairs? Follow me," he laughed some more as she huffed and playfully shoved his shoulder.

Walking back through the now darkening streets, they saw that the night life had begun. Lanterns and torches were hung outside of doors, posts, and on strings that dangled above the walkways. Couples walked by holding hands and snacks. The smell of different food venues filled the air with a delicious aroma. The stone steps leading up the mansion had lanterns on every step in black and red, casting dancing shadows. Mel wondered how they had all been there earlier or who had lit them all.

"Thanks, Daniel, it was fun. How about we finish the tour another time?" Mel asked. Swaying back and forth on her heels.

"That would be great," he held out his hand, "friends."

"Friends," she agreed, shaking his hand only to feel him slide something into it. It was the hand mirror, its silver gold surface sparkling in the night light, its flowers gleaming almost like magic. "I can't take this," she added, pushing it back toward him.

He shook his head, closing her hands around it. "Keep it. It's a sign of our friendship and a welcome present."

"Are you sure?" She asked again, meeting his soft brown eyes, feeling a small flutter in her chest. The look he gave her said he wouldn't take it back. "Well, see you later. Noches, Daniel."

"Noc-noc," he paused, giving a small cough, "night Melosia."

Daniel watched as she ran up the stairs attempting to take them two at a time. He covered his mouth to stifle a laugh when she stumbled turning to give him a cheeky thumbs up. Lowering his hand a bright green moth flew by getting caught in the flames of a lantern. In moments the once beautiful insect was extinguished.

Chapter 7

- -

Mel walked into the dining hall which had small groups sparsely spread about at the long tables. There were many different plates of meats, baskets of bread, and vegetables littered across the tables on red and gold embroidered table runners. She noticed Lupus sitting at the head of the longest table in a large chair. He signaled for her to sit in the seat to his left. To his right was the guy with purple hair, the one who caught her sneaking on the third floor. He looked at Lupus expectantly.

"Good evening, uncle," Mel said, pulling out the wooden chair.

"Likewise, how was your day?" He asked, taking a long sip from his tea cup.

Mel recounted the events of the day. How she explored and made a new friend. She pulled out the decorations for her room and told him what she planned to do with them. Lupus nodded and chimed in every few seconds. Taking a suspicious glance at the stranger that sat next to Lupus, she glossed over the fact that she had a brief encounter with him. The stranger seemed to take a light interest in her story as he sat drinking his tea with a refined grace.

"I promised to see Daniel again, we'd meet at one of the spots he showed me. Probably tomorrow. I can't wait for the adventures to come, what I'll see and do. When do we do whatever it is we do here?" She beamed, stretching her arms as she leaned into the high back of the chair.

"Not to rain on your parade but tomorrow, starts your training," Lupus stated, leaning onto the table.

"Training? What do you mean by training? Training was never mentioned."

"No offense, but you would die in five seconds if I released you out into the world. I'd rather not have your mother come after me with a machete so soon. You will be put through vigorous training before you are allowed to go on any type of adventure let alone leave this village," he explained, laughing heartily. Once his chuckles receded, he pointed at the purple-haired stranger. "And that is why he is the man of the hour. This is Johnathan, my right hand man, second in command, nanny, and your teacher. From tomorrow on, you will be in his capable hands."

"Hello, Melosia, it is nice to formally meet you ," Jonathan said, giving her a scrutinizing look.

"Mel, is just fine," she replied with a small tilt of her head.

"I think I'll leave you two alone to get to know each other a little better. But before I go, Mel, I need you to meet me here tomorrow morning. I'll give you a small orientation of how things are done here. It'll be quite an information dump so make sure not to stay up too late," Lupus winked and rose, walking to another small group.

A few minutes of silence passed after her uncle had taken his leave. Mel used the opportunity to pile a plate up and start munching.

Johnathan seemed to be waiting patiently for her to finish as he sat observing the other tables with dark blue eyes.

"Did my uncle just call you his nanny or was I just hearing things?" She inquired, wiping her face with a napkin.

"He did. He thinks it's funny leaving everything for me to do like a three your old that can't even tie his own boots," Johnathan replied, a cold bite in his words.

Mel opened her mouth, but then closed it not knowing how to reply. But she didn't have to worry, because it seemed the flood gates had opened as Johnathan started speaking again.

"Like today, for instance, instead of filing and signing the necessary documents that should have been done, not one, or two, but three weeks ago, he disappeared again, leaving it all for me to do on my own. I don't even know where he goes at this point. I have found all his other hiding places. And a few days ago when that demon just disappeared from our borders he said he handled it, but I don't trust his word. Don't take offense, but I hope for your own sake that your work ethic is better than that of Lord Lupus," he ranted, speech progressively getting faster, as he laced his fingers together and leaned toward her on the dark table.

"Yes, no, I mean I'm a hard worker," she stuttered, waving her hands frantically, face flushing.

Jonathan stared, seeming to gauge her reaction before nodding. He took one last sip from his cup, then rose, bid her good night, and left. She watched him go, deciding it would be best to follow suit for the massive lecture Lupus was supposed to give her in the morning. If she learned anything from school, it was that sleep is one of your best friends. Without sleep everything goes in one ear and not the other.

The next morning, in what Mel presumed was early dawn, she sat yawning at the dining hall table. Lupus had knocked on her door to wake her. The mansion was chilly with warm candle light that flickered and danced in the faces of the few occupants that sat about the room eating and talking. She hoped that the chill wasn't a sign of how cold the winters here would be as she breathed out a misty puff of air. The flames lit shadows around the room giving her uncle an eerie background for a storyteller. He leaned forward, resting his elbows on the table.

"The official name of this country is Rege but its original name, that everyone outside of the capital calls it, is Monstrum Terra. Sounds much cooler than Rege if you ask me. The original name dates back to when settlers, from a superstitious country far out in the sea, first set foot on this island. A simple name to describe what they saw, giant monsters."

"Monsters, like what's on the tapestries! What do they look like, do they still exist? Can I see one?!" Mel shot up, excitement waking her up completely at the thought of seeing monsters. Her imagination went wild with images and ideas.

"I'll get to it when I get there. I'm the one telling the story, and yes, like the tapestries. Can I continue now? Giant monsters roamed the land. The original founders decided upon a simple name of the beasts, demons. For these beasts were animals of vast size, had the intellect of humans, and were seemingly unkillable. Like most things we don't understand they related them to the supernatural calling them demons. The people fought for their new land with little success, until a boat with a group of mercenaries arrived from a small isle off the coast. These mercenaries claimed to know how to deal with the demons and used magic, traps, and tricks to fight the demons. Eventually, the demons became less of a menace and disappeared for a time."

"You see, everyone believed that the only trick the demons' had was their size, wit, and magic, but they had something else up their sleeves or should I say fur. They were shapeshifters in a sense, able to change their size, but more importantly, they could transform into humans. Problems arose from this and the first unholy union of demon and human occurred. The child seemed human enough but was stronger, faster, and had power that surpassed that of a normal human. These children when discovered were rooted out as abominations, but it got to the point that it was impossible to control. Eventually the mercenaries found a use for these children and took them in to train."

"A name was given to this new lifeform, you could say, and they came to be known as the animal tribes, based after the animal form their demon predecessor would take. Villages were built around these tribes and it became their duty to handle demons and monitor lands that the nobles didn't care for," he stopped, taking a hardy sip of coffee seemingly to have finished.

"Is that all?"

"Yes, all that is important."

"What about politics and the nobility?"

"That stuff doesn't matter out here. Only that we are members of the tribe. We fight demons and protect our land."

"That's all; I thought there would be more, there is more! You made a big deal out of it yesterday. How can you bring me here and not give me any information?!"

"Well, the tribes used to be numerous, but many have been on the decline, ours included. There are nasty rivalries between certain tribes and it led to their own downfall. There are only fourteen tribes left. I believe that is all you need to know at this time Johnathan will fill you in on the other details."

"What do you mean? What is the tribe we are a part of? Was my dad a dem-? No, he died; he couldn't have been, then mom, yup definitely mom, that explains so much," Mel muttered, nodding to herself a strong sense of understanding washing over her.

"Sorry to disappoint you, but Minerva is not a demon; she's as scary as one but not one. Demon blood is like a taint. It can go dormant and only appear in a select few of a bloodline. The demon of our blood line would be my father, and even though we shared the same father my brother did not inherit any of the demon blood. Instead the blood was passed on only to be inherited by you my great-niece. Also you should figure out what the tribe is on your own. Where is the fun in just being told everything?" He said, picking up a piece of bacon and eating it.

"Wait, wait, wait. Hold on a minute! What do you mean great-niece!?"

"You didn't know," he said, looking at her in surprise. "I'm Minerva's uncle. She never specified that, did she? My brother was your grandfather, making me your great uncle."

"No way, you can't be my great uncle. You look only a little older than mom."

"Nope, I'm your great uncle. Demon blood slows down the aging process a tad bit and my brother had Minerva young," he said matter of factly. "I think that is all the important information I want to impart on you today."

"What do you mean important? You've barely told me anything. This has been the most uninformative information dump ever. My head hurts now," she groaned, placing her head on the table in defeat.

"Now, now don't be like that. Johnathan will fill in the things I skipped over."

"You mean everything."

"Stubborn like your mother," he sighed, shaking his head with a grin. "Anyway, Johnathan will be here in a little while to take you, so eat while you still can. You see, training cuts into his already supposedly dense schedule so I apologize if he takes his stress out on you."

Mel sat, more confused than ever before. She reached over and scratched at the threads of the table runner, her mind fumbling. She was part demon or monster. Why would her mother never mention any of this; she had even lived here for her younger years. But most importantly why couldn't Lupus explain better? Was he hiding something? Huffing, she slumped back into her chair, threading her hands through her hair. *Eating is the only thing I can do*, she thought, grabbing a porcelain plate.

The dining hall had a steady stream of people coming in and out, and after some time, Johnathan arrived. Signaling, he had her follow him out to the training hall. He was silent for the small walk, deep in thought. She didn't mind as she was still mulling over the details of the conversation with her uncle, or great uncle if she wanted to be specific. No wonder people kepting making the old man joke.

"Training will be simple. We'll train every day. After every two days you get a break. Evidently Lord Lupus swears I'd kill you from over exhaustion if I had my own way," Johnathan explained once they arrived at the training hall. Mel stopped looking at the training swords to stare at him, trying to register if she heard him right or if he was humoring her. The serious set of his brow made her think he wasn't.

"Today will be an introductory day. First, warm up exercises, then a run, and then sparring. Dedication and discipline are the founding blocks of strength. As Lord Lupus explained, strength is important in this world, without it you'll be killed. I'll do everything I can to make you stronger, but it will be your choice if you survive or not. Understood."

"Yes?!"

For the next two hours Mel found herself doing warm up exercises. She laid on the cold floor with a disgusting layer of sweat sticking to her like a second set of clothing. Her breath came out in short heavy puffs and burned. For a simple warm up, it felt more to her like a full body work out for a marathon runner. Closing her eyes, she tried to suck up the chill from the floor by osmosis.

Johnathan stood peering at her with his one visible eye waiting for her to catch her breath. His expression was almost unreadable but she had a feeling that he was disappointed in her lack of physical ability. She pushed herself up on shaking elbows to a sitting position. Glancing at him, she tried her best to have a look of determination even if she wanted the earth to retake her at that moment.

"It would seem best to take a break for lunch and then continue," he rubbed his temples after a few minutes of thought.

Mel jumped to her feet and her head started spinning. Stumbling. She violently pin-wheeled her arms to regain her balance. Letting out a shaky breath, she glanced up to see Johnathan staring. She could have sworn she saw a flash of scorn in those eyes. She put her chin up high. Everyone gets light headed naturally. Only a weirdo wouldn't after a workout like that. Then again, she had been with Johnathan for less than a day and already she was questioning his origins as a human in general, demon blood included. Only someone not right in the head would think what he put her through was a beginner's warm up.

In the dining hall, Mel proceeded to unceremoniously shovel different meats and bread down her throat. Every few moments she had to stop to remember to breathe. She knew it was a horrible way to eat in public but she was famished and no amount of food would cut it.

"You know eating too fast and too much isn't good for the body," Johnathan stated with a grimace as she ate a biscuit in two bites, punching her chest to help her swallow.

"Sorry," she mumbles, turning away with a scowl. *Good thing it's not your body*, she thought, ripping into another bread.

When they finished eating, Johnathan led her outside the mansion and through the village, all the way to the large entrance gate that read in intricate gold letters Stella Luna. The dirt path led straight into the forest that surrounded the village. As they walked down the earthy path the smell of wood and detritus lingered in the air, getting stronger with each step. Many of the trees had already started to lose their leaves, becoming bare to the elements and wind. A ways off the path, she spotted a small farm with three wooden cabins. Eventually they stopped next to a large stream, its dirty brown water foaming and gurgling over the rocks. On the other side of the stream a large meadow opened up with tall brown grasses and dying wild flowers dotting the surface. A large shadow of a mountain rose in the distance like a foreboding titan.

"I'm going to show you the borders of our territory. You'll run the perimeter every day of training," Johnathan folded his arms behind his back, giving himself a self-important air.

"That should be easy," she muttered.

"We'll see about that. Now this stream serves as one of our borders. I'll lead you around the entire perimeter of our land. Just follow me," he said, taking off in a fast trot.

Despite acting like a stick in the mud, Mel learned her new teacher had a strange sense of humor. After making her run at a breakneck speed for ten minutes, he stopped for her to catch up. She fell over in a huff, laying on the earthy ground. The smell of dirt and rotting leaves filled her nose as she tried to catch her breath. The smirk on his face said it all. *That jerk!*

"Not so easy is it? We aren't even a fourth of the way through. I hope you understand now that this will be no walk in the park," he said, leaning over her. "In time you'll be able to handle this and more, if you follow my lead." He added, before disappearing.

Mel blinked two or three times to make sure her eyes had registered that correctly. Scrambling on her knees, she whipped her head to the right and left, scanning the area. He was gone. Had she eaten some weird mushroom for lunch? Maybe she had passed out and not realized it and he had abandoned her? A small panic bubbled in her stomach when it sank in that she was alone in an unknown wood. Her hair prickled on end at the normal sounds of wildlife rustling through the drying leaves. Nervously, she glanced around her again, anxiety washing over her in waves. If she just turned around and walked straight back, she should be alright. *No, we went off the path you idiot,* she thought, biting her thumb. Her racing thoughts were cut short by a chuckle overhead. Raising her dark eyes to the tree crown she saw Johnathan sitting on a low hanging branch.

"What the heck! I thought I had gone crazy! How'd you do that? Will I be able to?" She shouted in rapid succession, accusation and wonder blending together.

"I'm sorry I couldn't help myself. My fat...father," he paused to jump down, coughing to clear his throat, "my father played a similar trick on me once. I just jumped and you will be able to do it with time. Now follow me. I'll go slower this time."

"Your father, what's he like?" She asked, jogging behind him after a few minutes. Silence followed as she watched his purple hair bounce ahead.

"Focus on training right now," was his terse reply as he jogged ahead through the underbrush.

Mel followed in silence. Something would scurry into the underbrush, catching her eye. She caught a glimpse of another two farms as they moved. The beauty of the outdoors would have been much more enjoyable if it weren't for the fact her lungs were on fire. Doubling over, she leaned on her knees to catch her breath. Some movement to her side got her attention. She glanced over and saw what might be a large dog slip into the shadows out of sight. A knot formed in her stomach and she glanced up to make sure that Johnathan had stopped for her, he had. She started moving again only to yelp and jump to the side when the stick she stepped on moved. The small brown snake watched her with curious eyes before slithering away as she held a hand to her chest.

"Scared of snakes?" Johnathan asked, placing a hand on her shoulder.

"No. Not, the small ones, and it startled me. Let's finish this," she replied, making a fist; she wouldn't be defeated by a simple jog in the woods. That would be too pathetic.

If not being able to jog at a decent pace was pathetic, Mel didn't know how to describe her current experience. Maybe being an amoeba. Because what Johnathan had described as a simple sparring match to test her reflexes was a boldfaced lie. At least she finally understood how a pinata felt. She lay on the floor, feeling sore with battered fingers barely touching the wood of the staff that had failed her once again. *Simple beginners training, my butt*, she cursed in her head, gritting her teeth to rise for another assault.

"I believe that is enough for the day. You are dismissed," Johnathan said, and to Mel it was the words of an angel. That is until he ruined it.

"And since today was just introductory it won't count on the schedule so we'll train an extra day before your break."

Mel felt the blood drain from her face. If this is what he considered introductory, what could possibly be considered a normal day? She stared at the floor, her feet sore and muscles aching like never before.

He's the devil, she thought, cursing his existence.

Chapter 8

Mel found herself in a long dark hallway, her steps echoing against the stone floor. A warm breeze blew down the corridor, carrying a whisper of her name. She followed the call, tense, as the darkness enveloped her. A soft whisper in her ear made her spin to the left to find a single door that had appeared out of the darkness. She opened the door with a creak, and her hair flew back with a sudden warm breeze. Oddly, another pair of doors greeted her. They were black with gold patterns. Kneeling in front of the doors, she peeked through the keyhole into still darkness. A red eye appeared from the gloom, jolting her backward. She was falling now into the darkness. The floor had vanished. She heard her name as the darkness consumed her.

With a shock, Mel awoke upon the hard cold floor. Her right leg is the only thing still touching the bed being tangled in the silk sheets. Releasing a groan, she rose, and curled back into the bed. Shaking her head to forget the strange dream, she let tiredness overtake her.

Melosia had never felt exhaustion like she did when she woke again. Forcing her eyes to open was a chore. Rubbing the sleep from them, she felt small twinges of pain prickle through her whole being. *Just two more days, then you can rest,* she chanted in her head repeatedly like a prayer. Maybe Johnathan had been so intense yesterday just to gauge her skills and lay the groundwork for the rest of her training and it would be easier now. She honestly hoped her new teacher was not a devil incognito. She wanted to like Johnathan. He was only a couple of years her senior, she hoped they could become friends.

Mel stared blankly at the small plate of fruits in front of her. Upon entering the dining hall, Johnathan had placed it before her. She blinked owlishly, staring at the meager meal of fruits and dried meat. Hunger gnawed at her stomach. She understood what the plate meant but didn't want to believe it. She glanced at his face with the question on her lips that she didn't want to utter and make real.

"From now on, I will monitor what you eat. You'll be going on a diet to help with your training. You might hate me now, but you will thank me later," was all he said before walking briskly away.

Mel wanted to protest, but didn't want to risk making him angry in case he made her training even more difficult, so instead, she bitterly cursed him in her head. Chewing on a small tough piece of ham she swore she would have her revenge.

"Good morning," a voice rang out next to Mel, she couldn't help but wonder if it was after Johnathan. She rolled her eyes and gave a jerky nod.

"Can I sit here? I'm sorry about what happened the other day. When I'm on a mission, I tend to put on the blinders," the woman said, pulling out the wooden chair with a grating screech.

Mel glanced at the new-comer. She had tanned skin, short, white hair in a pixie cut, and bright eyes, the color of molten gold. If Mel had met this woman before she would have remembered her.

Pushing the fruit around with a tarnished fork, Mel's lip twitched. "Sorry, but I think you have the wrong person."

"Nope. You're old man Lupus' niece, right? I ran you over a few days ago," she closed her eyes with a large grin.

"What? Wait!" Mel lept from her seat, wincing at the pain in her legs, and pointed a shaking finger at her. "You're the brute that plowed into me my first day here!"

The woman lifted her hands in a pleading manner. "Guilty as charged. The name is Tsume; if you need anything in the future, don't hesitate to ask."

"I'll definitely remember that," was her gruff reply.

"Don't be moody. I want you to see me as a big sister," she threw an arm around Mel's neck, pulling her close. The action caused Mel to drop her grape. She gave a forlorn look as it rolled away under the table.

"Tsume, please refrain from harassing my student," Johnathan said, walking over.

"No wonder you're moody. Anyone would after getting the Johnathan death sentence," She laughed, smacking Mel on the back, making her almost drop her juice. The orange liquid sloshed sloppily over the edge.

"And what is that supposed to mean?" He asked, visibly confused.

"I don't know, maybe the fact that any disciple you take under your wing quits and runs away in tears less than a week later. I think the longest record is a week and a half."

"That is...I mean. Strength is needed to survive and they just didn't have what it takes," He said, crossing his arms.

"Kid, you never change. Always too extreme. Now, Mel, if he goes too far, just tell me and I'll put him in a nice headlock," she winked before ruffling their hair and leaving.

"If you have finished eating, we should start training," he said in a terse tone.

Any hope Mel had that the day before had just been a test were dashed and smashed to a billion pieces. The day's training was just as rough, maybe even worse if she took into account her exhaustion from the day before. Cuts and scratches littered her arms and legs from running through briers. Her clothes were ruined, covered in small smudges of blood and mud, and were sopping wet, chilling her to the bone. She had slipped in the woods and plunged into the brown stream's icy water. Clawing herself back up the slick muddy bank had been no easy task. When Johnathan appeared she had hoped it was to help her up he just watched as she struggled, sliding back in with a wet splash. Sweat burned her eyes as it poured from her brow while sparring with the mad-man. The staff struck painfully with a loud smack almost every second. One particularly nasty blow to the stomach had her double over, retching violently. As she gagged and choked, she truly believed he wanted to kill her.

Once he released her, she locked herself away in her room; Mel collapsed onto her bed. It felt like she had not slept in years. Her body burned and aches all over. Even soaking in the warm porcelain bathtub from the heated plumbing brought only the slightest of comfort. What had she gotten herself into? She wanted an adventure, not hellish training. Her goal was fun and adventure not agonizing pain. Wrapping the blanket around herself, she closed her eyes and let sleep take hold of her.

Like a zombie, Mel chewed on her morning biscuit. She hurt all over but wasn't going to let that stop her. If she quit what would that mean, failure, and she didn't want to have to go through that especially the look of disappointment and hurt in her mother's eyes. Failure was never an option. She kept thinking that it would get easier with time that she just had to get used to it; mind over matter. Munching on her single piece of bacon, she glanced up to meet the eyes of a red headed boy who looked away quickly. Thinking nothing of the boy, she stood up to head to training, only to hear a chair hastily scrape across the floor.

"Excuse me, who are you? I'm Reginald," the red head inquired, his amber eyes seeming to judge her for some strange reason. His sharp eyes and slicked back hair gave him a severe look like that of an arrogant honor student.

"Melosia, but Mel is fine," she replied, not liking how his eyes bore into her.

"How pathetic. You look like a drowned dog and you have only been here, what three days? It is always the same. Someone thinks they are good enough to train under Johnathan's genius tutelage only to flee like a spineless coward!" He sneered, looking down his nose at her.

"Excuse me?!"

"You heard me. Between you and me I don't care if you are our leader's flesh and blood. A pathetic little girl will always be a little girl. You should just go back to where you came from. Honestly, people like you don't even understand what an honor it is to train under someone of Johnathan's stature."

"What do you know about me, you jerk? I don't even know you."

"I'm the one person who respects Johnathan and you clearly do not, I can see it in your eyes. I bet you won't last very long, probably begging to go back home to mommy in a couple of days," he shrugged, walking away, leaving Mel irritated and a little confused.

Everyone has those days when they are fueled purely by spite. For Mel, that day was here. She did her morning exercises with passion and took off into the woods; although she may have thrown her lunch up from over-exertion. She even gave a valiant effort in sparring; though she still ended up feeling like a sad little pinata. It didn't help that that jerk had appeared, not only during lunch to continuously sneer at her from across the room, but during the sparring match as well. She swore she heard that miscreant snicker at her pain. She would show Reginald, *he will pay for incurring my latina wrath*, she thought, punching a training dummy and wincing.

A slow clap had Mel turn furiously on her heels, ready to punch who-ever dared mock her in the training hall only to see Tsume's grin. She strolled over to the smaller girl, took her hands in her own and started to move her around like a marionette.

Once Tsume had finished, she nodded in triumph. "That is the best stance for someone of your stature. How about I teach you a few techniques? Maybe you could use them for some stress relief, you probably need it."

Mel nodded in dazed wonder, deciding that she probably liked this lady more now. The rest of the evening she spent learning simple punching and kicking stances. A wicked smirk inched its way on her face as she thought how she would prove that vile redhead wrong.

Chapter 9

Gazing up at the bright sky with its fluffy clouds, Mel knew it was a good day. She stretched her sore arms up, reaching out her fingers, causing her joints to pop. Sleeping in was a good way to start her rest day. She hopped down the stone steps, wondering what she should do for the day, but then she remembered that she meant to spend some time with Daniel. It would be nice to be with a person that wasn't making her do outrageous exercises or trying to pick a fight in the first few minutes of meeting her. And speaking of pains in her side, once she stepped off the last step, she heard a familiar snide voice.

"What do you want, stupido?" She asked, picking up her pace to make it to one of the places Daniel said he hung around.

Reginald easily fell into step with her. "Stupid-what? Name calling is quite immature. I just wanted to see how you would spend your valuable day off. And I see you squandering it, how very much like you."

"No offense, but how I spend my time is none of your business," she retorted, seething as she thought of some Spanish insults to use.

He sneered as Daniel came running up. "I guess losers tend to be drawn to each other. I can't wait for another great display of your ability tomorrow." After a small bow, he turned on his heel, shooting a look of disdain.

"Please don't," Mel groaned, rubbing her temples.

"What was that about?" Daniel asked, cocking his head.

"Just getting harassed by el chupacabra."

"That's why Reginald was with you, I should have guessed. He treats me pretty badly too; he wasn't that bad until he learned I was friends with John. Speaking of John, how's the training going? And what did you call Reginald?" He smiled, scratching the back of his head.

"Oh man, after just three days I feel like a different person; a mere shell of the old me," she replied darkly. "El chupacabra it's a goat blood sucking monster. I called Reginald one because he sucks!"

"That sounds about right for both. John goes to the extreme when it comes to training. I know! How about I take you horse riding today? I'll help you saddle the mare up and everything," he clapped his hands together in glee. He was so happy about the idea that Mel didn't have the heart to deny him.

The two walked to the barn, passing by the clanging of the black-smiths, the air thick with smoke. Inside the wooden stables Daniel showed Mel how to tighten and place the saddle, and the bridle and reins. Mel wanted to try and do it all herself declaring that she didn't need help much to his amusement. The light tan mare, Sandy, nick-ered and whined as Mel placed the saddle on over the blanket securing all the buckles and straps. Stepping back she took a look at her handy work and smirked at Daniel with a nod of pride.

"Just take the reins and we'll lead them out to the woods," he said, leading the way from the stable through the dirt roads of the village, waving every now and then at the passersby.

Making it to the front gates, Daniel put his hands out to prop Mel onto the saddle. She tensed immediately as the saddle and horse moved causing her to sway. The mare took a few steps forward as Daniel got onto his chestnut colored horse, and he rode in front, instructing her how to use the reins.

"Yes, just like that. We'll go nice and slow, just scope out the area," he grinned as they took the horses at a lazy pace.

"Is training that soul crushing?" He joked, after some peaceful silence with only the sound of crushing leaves under hoof to accompany them.

"It is in fact satanic and spartanic; and honestly I think a part of my soul has actually died from overexertion. You might have seen it when it ascended to the heavens last night," she replied, lifting an arm up toward the distance with a forlorn gaze, causing him to snort.

The two continued to ride out slowly, chatting every now and then. It was a new experience and Mel actually enjoyed it all: The feeling of the crisp fall breeze, the small scurrying of squirrels in the underbrush, and the sound of singing birds. It was a shock when the world went horizontal as she crashed into a bush. She lay stunned blinking as she stared at Sandy and the saddle that now lay on the underside of her belly. A fit of laughter brought her out of her stupor.

Daniel sat trembling on his horse trying in vain to hold in his laughter. Fresh tears started to form as he gave into the fit. Mel flushed, grabbing a small dry twig, then slinging it at him. He ducked to the side as the twig flew harmlessly into the underbrush as he continued to laugh. He slid off his steed, and walked over to her, extending one hand while wiping his eyes with the other. Puffing out her cheeks, she grabbed his hand and stood to dust herself off.

"Will you stop laughing, it's not funny," she snapped, placing her hands on her hips.

"I'm sorry, it's just, your face when you fell. It was like, huh, I'm falling, and then you fell!"

"Oh, so now my face is funny. I warned you," she pulled up her foot ready to take off her boot.

"No, anything but that chanclata! You know that's not what I meant."

"It's chancleta, and you are on thin ice. I'm warning you."

By the time Daniel stopped laughing, Mel was already on the horse and starting back down the trail. He followed, close behind, trying in vain to start up another conversation as she huffed. Staring at the saddle, he was about to tell her that she should tighten the straps when yet again the saddle slipped under the mare's belly causing the girl to fall off. This time, Daniel jumped off the horse and leapt to her side when she released a small yelp.

A painful splinter was jammed into Mel's index finger from the branch she grabbed when she fell. She let out a soft hiss then tried to remove it, but couldn't pinch it out making her release a few choice spanish words. She tried using her teeth but the cursed splinter was buried just under the skin. Sighing, she tried to close her hand, only to feel it prickle in pain. *Hopefully, I can endure this irritation until the splinter becomes one with my body*, she thought grimacing.

"Let me see," Daniel siad, taking her hand and examining it. "It's in there good. We're going to have to cut it out."

"Cut?!" She shrieks, snatching her hand back and cradling it to her chest. Splinters and knives did not go well together in her mind.

"Come on, it won't hurt; a tiny nick and no more irritating pain," he replied, producing a small knife with a wooden handle from his back pocket.

Daniel took her hand again much to her displeasure. She glared at the knife as its shimmering blade got closer. Once the blade almost touched her skin, she let out a scream causing him to jerk back and stare at her eyes wide.

"Sorry, I don't like the idea of pain," she mumbled shyly, a faint blush spreading over her cheeks.

"Don't worry. You gave me quite a fright there, though," he said, placing a hand over his chest. "Hey, if it's scary, close your eyes. It will be over in a second, I promise. If I hurt you, I'll let you cut my finger," he added. He looked so kindly at her it made her heart skip a beat.

Mel nodded, scrunching up her eyes. She braced herself for pain but just like he said and like every time her father would do the same thing, it was just a small quick sting. She cracked open one eye to see the cursed splinter gone. She saw Daniel had gone to her mare and was adjusting the saddle straps. She started to open her mouth, the tip of a question on her tongue, when he turned to her with a smile.

"That should do it. The strap was loose, making the saddle slip. You shouldn't fall anymore. Want to continue or head back?"

"I'm a bit hungry. Let's head back."

"How are you adjusting? Is it that different here?" Daniel asked.

Mel turned her head to the side, mulling over his question. "Sorry the only thing I can think of is school and electricity. I don't miss school but I do miss tv," she laughed scratching her head.

Daniel snorted. "You're from another dimension and that's the only thing you can think of."

"I like the food here too."

"You're not helping your case," he smiled, pulling up closer to her. "Tell me about this tv you miss."

"I guess you'd describe it as moving pictures on a screen. I miss watching my shows with Alma, my little sister. We watch this comedy cartoon called Knights of the Night, this'll be the first time we'll miss watching it together," she said gazing at the leather reins in her hands. Her shoulders sagged as she sighed from the small pit that formed in her stomach. "We watch everything together," she added in a soft whisper.

"Tell me about the show," he said, attempting to bring a smile back to her face.

Mel beamed at him before rattling off the story in a twisting narrative that kept backpedaling from her forgetting plot points or having to introduce whole character stories. She could tell that Daniel was completely lost, but kept listening all the same, warming her heart. He smiled at her childish excitement.

They paused when the horses ears went back and they whinnied in distress as they stamped their hooves. The bushes further up the trail were shaking.

Mel looked at Daniel in concern. A large gray wolf padded out. Terror and awe gripped her simultaneously as her stomach dropped. Would it attack them? The wolf stared at them with intelligent yellow eyes, then made a yep, and a group of three fur balls ran out from behind. The wolf waited for all the pups to cross the path before cocking its head in the riders' direction and following the pups.

Mel waved a hand in excitement mouthing the words 'so cute' as Danel nodded in agreement. They continued their ride to the village. They ate a small dinner on their return, then said their goodbyes for the night.

"You're going to need all the extra rest you can get. If you thought the first days were tough, you're in for a rude awakening. John will ramp up the pace at some point, and the more rest you get, the better. I'd hate for any more of your soul to be killed." He snickered. Mel smacked his shoulder when he whispered. "Or pride. I know you'll do great. Give it all you got!"

"Thanks, I'll take you at your word. Noches!" She smiled, beginning to walk up the stone staircase to the dark looming mansion. After a few steps she paused and turned to him. "Let's go riding again, but next time you handle the saddles," she added with a quick wave.

Chapter 10

When Daniel had warned Mel about Johnathan ramping up the pace, she was not prepared for it to be in the form of weights. Morning exercising with arm and leg weights, running through the wilderness with heavier leg weights, and now sparring with ankle weights. By now the clunky weights had rubbed her skin raw. Gritting her teeth, she prepared for another assault. Johnathan had also decided that for sparring she would be on defense only for the time being; she was sure it was because of how pathetic the last matches had gone.

Johnathan walked a lazy circle around her as she stood clutching the staff in front of her. She stepped slowly, keeping her eyes on him at all times trying to gauge any sign of movement, like he had instructed her to. She blinked. In a flash he was on her. He spun the staff in a graceful arc striking her in the back of the knees. Jamming her own staff into the floor, she tried to keep balance. But the move cost her as four consecutive hits to the neck, back, side, and stomach followed, leaving her a heaving heap on the floor.

As she lay there panting. Johnathan sat cross legged in front of her, waiting. Upon regaining her breath, she sat up and watched him suspiciously. His staff lay off to the side and the relaxed way he was sitting didn't make a surprise attack seem likely. *Is this a test*, she wondered, fingers tightening around the smooth surface of the staff next to her. She whipped her arm out as fast as she could muster. He caught it with his bare hand without even blinking.

"A decent attempt for a sneak attack, but you'll need more practice. Your eyes gave it away," he said, yanking the staff from her fingers. "I think it's time for a small lesson on our customs. Today, it will be magic."

"Magic! Will I be able to shoot lightning from my eyes?" She asked, rocking back and forth, a new sense of excitement giving her a rush of much needed energy.

"Um, no," he replied, staring at her incredulously.

"Then what's the point?" She huffed, crossing her arms.

"Magic is a potent force. As a tribe member, you are naturally attune to an element, whereas a magician must learn to use items to cast spells to harness the elemental spirits of nature."

"Only two types of people can use magic, then?"

"Correct, in a sense. A magician has a natural affinity to the spirits of nature, while tribe members inherited the ability from their demon lineage. So yes, before you ask, demons can also use a magical element, leading to a theory from scholars that demons were originally nature spirits that took on physical form. Now it is important that you know that if a female has a significantly high affinity for the elements of nature, she is considered an elementalist and a fortune teller, because she has an acute sixth sense. Her hunches are normally accurate. Meaning, if Lady Cornelia gives you advice, it is best to follow it."

"Wait a second! The bear was taken by plants. I swore my head was messing with me but was that real? Was it Uncle?"

"No, that was Lady Cornelia. Her strongest affinity is to plant life though she can use almost any element if she wants."

"How did she teleport us? Could she shoot flowers from her eyes if she wanted too?"

Johnathan rubbed his temples. "Space and time are considered elements of the strongest kind, since Lady Cornelia is an exceptional elementalist; teleportation is in her power. She can't do it often because the task is taxing on her energy. For a second time no shooting an element from your eyes is not possible."

"When do we start then? When can I learn?" She sat up straight, rubbing her hands together with glee.

"It's too soon. You'd die if you attempted magic in your state right now. You'd be completely overwhelmed by the spirits, and die a terrible death."

"That's not fair, why bring it up then?" she whined, crossing her arms and in a hushed voice added. "Not like anything has stopped you from attempting to murder me every other day."

"Knowledge is always a firm foundation," he said, pacing with his arms behind his back before turning to her with a soft smile. "It is also a great segue into starting meditation."

While they meditated, Reginald stalked into the training hall. His presence was a thorn in her side making it hard to concentrate. Johnathan rose, telling her training was over and to get her ankles checked later, before leaving. As she was exiting the room she heard a snide mumble and turned on the red head.

"You want to go, Chupacabra?" she snarled, clenching her fist.

"I thought you would never ask. Anything to put you in your place would be fun," he replied, kicking up two of the wooden staffs. He caught them both and threw one to her.

She caught it with a sigh of relief and started to stalk forward. "Bring it, Chupacabra."

"Alright, princess," he gave a sarcastic bow.

Mel took the opening, lashing for his exposed side. He ducked under the blow with amazing flexibility. Like a cat, he pounced on her, pushing her back with a flurry of blows. After a few moments it was clear he was playing with her, the way he was dancing around her before striking. She made a desperate attempt to strike him. He released his own staff and caught her, twisting it making her arm snap to the side in a painful angle. In a flash his hand was on the back of her head and his knee pressing into the small of her back as she lay on the floor, pinned. She felt a warm breath on her ear as he leaned close to her.

"This chupa-whatever still whipped the floor with you, princess. Remember that," he sneered before rising, turning to Johnathan, who had just walked back into the training hall.

"If you would like, I can spar more with her. It'll be good for her to have someone more on her level." He paused, giving her a sneer. "To compete with."

Johnathan stared at him for a few moments before giving a small smile. "Thank you for the suggestion, Reginald, that would be help-ful," he said, turning away.

Reginald nodded but before he left he gave Mel a smile that made her skin crawl with disgust and contempt. The jerk just wanted to mess with her. She could see the malice in his golden eyes.

Mel sat up, rubbing her arm and grumbling. She headed to the in-firmary like Johnathan had suggested after she stopped her pity party.

Storm handled her gently with kind, gold eyes, though she might have gone a bit too far bandaging Mel's ankles saying it's best to be careful. The bandages were thick and scratchy when all she needed to do was slap a band-aid on it and call it a day.

In her bed Mel tugged and readjusted the tick cotton wrapping her ankles. She had spent some time removing the excess fabric that wasn't needed. Storm had believed that the bandages should go higher than needed to stay secure. After trimming the fabric, Mel tucked the now shortened end into the wrap. From now on, longer socks. *Lesson learned*, she thought in a self-deprecating way, releasing a small snort.

"I heard you had to go to the infirmary yet again last night," Reginald said, taking a seat across from Mel in the dining hall. "Is it from me wiping the floor with you yesterday, or did you have an accident on the way to bed, princess?"

Mel just stared at him as she brought a piece of melon to her mouth and bit into it. She wasn't in the mood to deal with him this early in the morning. The last week of him 'helping' with training had been hell. Her body hurt all over even in places she didn't think should be hurting and an extra pain in the butt was not needed. Taking a swig of juice, she locked her eyes with him, pretending to look right through him. His jaw clenched and he scrunched up his nose.

"Ignoring me, very mature." His lip twitched into a smirk. He leaned forward onto the table to get closer to her. She didn't like the look in his eyes.

"You know from what I've heard from Lord Lupus, that you wanted to come here. Going as far as running away from home. What kind of person abandons their family without any thought. Are you running away from something? Thought it would be fun here and play make believe. I give you one more day before you have a breakdown and run back home."

"I'll say it again-what do you even know about me?" she asked, shooting him a glare and resisting the deep urge to smash her creamy potato soup into his face.

"I've seen enough from how you carry yourself to make a safe assumption about your character."

"And what would that be?"

"That a failure is always a failure. No matter how hard you try, nothing will change. You're not one of us, you're just a weak little mouse scurrying away from things when they get too hard. I don't know why Lord Lupus would think you'd make a good replacement for Johnathan."

"That's not true at all and I don't want Johnathan's job. What would make you even think of that?"

"I've heard lots of rumors, but most of them say that Lord Lupus only brought you here to adopt you as his heir and to replace Johnathan. Oh, did that hurt to hear your uncle only sees you as a pawn. Well, later mouse princess." He shrugged, walking away with a smug grin plastered on his face.

Mel gritted her teeth. She stabbed into her remaining fruit with fury. What he said hurt and was wrong. Her uncle wasn't using her as a pawn, he was weird but always kind to her. And what did Reginald know she was trying her hardest. This week he had bullied her and tormented her every time Johnathan's back was turned. She had tried to use the pointers Tsume had given her but she was too weak. She dug her nails into her palms to stop the tears that prickled at the corners of her eyes. *I'll show that jerk*, she thought with bitter resentment.

She pinched the bridge of her nose, taking a deep breath. She thought of peaceful things; her mom and sister, riding her bike, and the few horse rides she'd taken with Daniel. Thinking of Daniel made her want to try harder because of the encouragement he gave her. She swallowed her last piece of fruit, feeling a buzz of energy replacing the malaise that Reginald had inspired.

But the problem with words is that once an idea forms in one's head, it is hard to get rid of it. Especially when it hits home.

For the rest of the day, Mel tried to block out Reginald's hateful words, but they kept nagging at the back of her mind like a gnat. She kept thinking about it over and over, her mind even adding more hurtful things. By the end of the day when she was sparring with Johnathan, she had all but convinced herself that she was the lowest of the low, an amoeba that was nothing in the grand scheme of things. She felt like she was being held up by a fraying rope on its final worn thread.

After the tenth or so failed block that resulted in a smack on the back, Mel collapsed and didn't get back up. She clenched her teeth and dug her nails into the floor, willing herself to get up, to keep trying, but the small fraying rope of her resolve had snapped. Who cared about any of this anyway? Who cares? Angry, red hot tears burned her eyes as they started to stream down. Sitting up, she made a vain attempt to wipe them away. Her breath came out in ragged gasps as she tried to calm herself. It was no use, the flood gates had opened, the stress her body had gone through, her mental state, and her doubts all crashed down on her. A gentle hand caressed her head. She glanced up through bleary eyes to see Johnathan patting her head.

"What's wrong? Something has been bothering you all day. Calm down first then tell me," he said, cutting her off when she attempted to start babbling incoherently.

"You know the saying, snitches get stitches? Well, that doesn't matter today, because that jerk keeps bullying me," Mel snapped, finally calming her tears. She took a deep breath and recounted all that Reginald had said and done over the past week. All the snide and backhanded comments, the taunts, the stalking, the sneering. It all came out like a raging torrent. Strangely, as she talked she felt a weight lift from her chest. Finishing her tirade she rubbed at her red eyes yet the tears wouldn't seem to stop.

"Being critical is fine to a point, but he went too far this time. I'll speak to him. Training is over for the day. Go try to rest," Johnathan said after thinking for some time and kneeling next to her. "And Melosia, you are the best student I've ever had. If you need me for anything, don't hesitate to ask for help," he added with a small smile, ruffling her hair gently.

Mel sat on her bed lazily opening and closing the silver hand mirror Daniel had gotten for her on his village tour. The bags under her eyes were frightening, like a cruel joke waiting to happen. It was still early since Johnathan cut training short but maybe she should get some extra sleep while she could. A sharp rapping on her door brought her out of her stupor. *Who could that be?* It would be odd for anyone to visit her unless it was her uncle. The repeated knocking sounded almost irritated. Rubbing the back of her neck, she opened the door, revealing the last person she wanted to see at this point; a roach would have been a more welcome sight than the redhead standing awkwardly at her door, holding a cantaloupe.

Mel attempted to slam the door without even exchanging a word but Reginald stuck his foot out just in time to stop it. She gritted her teeth as she tried in vain to smash his foot with the door as he curled his fingers around the door to keep it open. Their standoff lasted for only seconds before he succeeded in wrenching the door open, making her stumble and land on her rear.

"What do you want?" she asked, dusting herself off.

"I've come to apologize for my earlier behavior." He turned and walked away, then paused, glancing over his shoulder to signal for her. "Follow me. Just come on."

Mel stood for a few seconds, and against her better judgment, followed Reginald down the long corridor. They walked in silence all the way to the third floor and up a small metal twirling staircase hidden behind a door. At the top of the stair-case, he opened another door. A soft breeze ruffled their hair as they stepped out onto a small platform on the roof with an iron railing. He sat down and gazed up at the sky, without a glance at her. *I guess we're not having that heart to heart talk,* she thought. With what felt like the hundredth sigh of the day, she followed suit and watched the setting sun descending down upon the earth as the sky bled with orange and pink hues.

Looking down from their perch onto the streets made the people that were scattered below look like ants. As the sky darkened, small lights appeared along the roads and paths from the lighting of lanterns. Some lights danced and bounced, appearing like will-o'-the-wisp or fallen spirits.

Reginald pulled out a knife and Mel wondered why she came up here with him in the first place but he passed it to her along with a small melon. She held it in her hand, the rough skin brushing against her fingers.

The thick tension that surrounded them was smothering. "What's with the melon?" she finally asked, not being able to take the silence any longer.

"It's a peace offering. Johnathan told me to apologize and I thought a gift would work well. I thought since your name was Mel you had to like melons." He said, not taking his eyes off the village's skyline.

"Ah. Should I be concerned that you might try to throw me off the rooftop, because I got you in trouble with Johnathan? You know, since you have that weird man-crush on him and all," she joked, cutting into the melon. Its sweet scent filled the crisp evening air.

Reginald stared at her incredulously before speaking. "No, I do not have a crush on Johnathan, I just admire him. And, no, I am not planning on throwing you from the roof-top. It would be much too obvious. I'd have more subtlety than that."

"You could have fooled me," she muttered, eating a slice.

"What is that supposed to mean?!" he snapped, as she looked away, pretending like she had not heard him.

"Fine, I'll explain. When I was younger-"

"Wait, are you about to tell me about your tragic back-story? Because, no offense, I don't care much for you or it." She cut him off, matter of factly pointing the knife at him.

"That was a very rude thing to say."

"Coming from you, that's hilarious. Pot calling the kettle black."

"I apologized already. Fine, I'm sorry again. I just get a little testy when it comes to Johnathan. When I was younger I took my little sisters out over our border and we were attacked. Johnathan saved us; it was amazing to know someone a few years older than me could be that reliable. So ever since then I've idolized him," he explained, rushing through the words to make sure that he was not cut off again. "Can I have a piece?" he added, slouching.

"No, you can't," she snapped.

"And why not?"

"Because I ate it all and regret it," she replied with one hand over her mouth from a small wave of nausea.

"You ate that whole thing! How?"

"Really fast, alright! Don't remind me."

Reginald stood to lean over the iron railing and gazed off into the distance in silence. Mel wondered if he was now planning on tossing her over it. She glanced at the door. She might make it, but with the over full feeling and stomach ache the odds were stacked against her. He would catch her in an instant, curse that cantaloupe and her poor impulse control. She jumped when he snapped his head in her direction.

"You might be trained by Johnathan, but I won't lose to you, you hear me? I'll be better than you in every way. Nothing you ever do will change that," he declared, standing tall. "From here on out, I won't apologize for my actions either."

Mel met his eyes and saw the passion in them; the challenge. She stood up with her hands on her hips. Turning her chin up high, she glared back at him.

"Bring it on, chupacabra, I'm not going to lose."

With that declaration of war, she spun on her heels and took her leave.

"I wouldn't have it any other way, princess."

Chapter 11

Swearing to beat Reginald had put a flame of passion into Mel's morning exercises. The days and weeks started to blur by as the seasons changed. She started to gain muscle and skill in defensive combat. The exhaustion from constant training and the bitter cold snow that she was not used to, gave her odd dreams. Often she dreamed of being a child again and playing with a black fox, when she'd awakened the feeling of nostalgia from the dream made her wonder if she had played with a fox before and couldn't remember.

Just recently, Johnathan had graduated her from only defense to actual combat in their sparring. He even started self-defense lessons. She didn't want to sound braggy, but Mel thought she took to these lessons quite well. Jonathan must have been pleased with her progress because he changed her diet to one she was much more accustomed to.

Another thing about the self-defense lessons was that, every other lesson, Tsume would drop in to give Mel pointers. Today was one of those days. Johnathan stood to the side rifling through a stack of papers while the two circled slowly. Mel focused on matching Tsume's slow pace and anticipating her moves. The rules of these matches were simple: exchange blows, and the first to get four clean hits wins. To this day, Mel: zero, Johnathan and Tsume: every victory, Reginald bet against her whenever he was allowed to show up and those losses were the worst, but today would be the day that she would succeed. She knew they went easy on her and it hurt what little pride she had left.

Tsume turned on her heel, changing her direction and Mel copied quickly. Their eyes locked and it was on. Tsume spun on her toes, lashing out her other leg in a kick. Mel squatted to maintain her balance, blocking the kick with her arm. Using her other hand, she grabbed Tsume's leg, hitting it the best she could. Tsume jumped onto her hands, twisting her body and wrenching her leg from the girl's hands with such finesse and force it was astounding. She then spun on her hands, spinning into a leg sweep.

Mel was ready, Tsume was fond of this maneuver and had performed it multiple times in the past. She jumped up just in time. But she wasn't prepared for how fast Tsume lunged onto her feet and drove four consecutive punches to her stomach, arms, and leg, taking her down in a blink of an eye. She hit the ground in frustration and gritted her teeth.

"Another?!" Mel half asked and half demanded between heavy pants, pointing to the ceiling. She wanted desperately to break this losing streak, even if it would be a fluke. Victory would be hers this day!

Tsume flashed a wide grin, dropping back into a fighting stance, but was stopped by Johnathan placing a hand on her shoulder. He handed her the papers he had been flicking through, with a shake of his head.

"No, that will be enough for the day. Thank you, Tsume for your help. Could you take these to Lord Lupus, if you please?" He turned to Mel. "Remember when we talked about magic? It should be time to test your element out."

"Yes! I can finally shoot lightning from my eyes?" Mel asked, jumping up and down.

"Can people do that where you're from?" Tsume asked, a spark of interest flashing through her eyes.

"No, unfortunately." Mel deflated, rubbing the back of her head.

Tsume frowned and shrugged, then took her leave. She waved with the papers and threw a mischievous wink in their direction. Johnathan sighed, walking to the side of the room near one of the weapon stands and picking up a small crystal ball.

"I'll demonstrate how this test goes. You just meditate, hold the ball and let your energy flow into it." He sat cross-legged, clutching the ball gently in his hands. The glassy surface started to mist as a ghostly blue light lit up the inside. The color swirled beneath the surface, reminding Mel of the water under the frozen stream in the woods.

Johnathan handed the ball to Mel. He walked away, saying something about getting a chart in case the vision was anything unique. The glass felt heavy in her hands, its surface cold and smooth. She did as she had for months now and calmed her breath, centering herself. Inhaling and exhaling in a slow rhythm. Watching the surface of the glass in anticipation and a bit of anxiety. *What if nothing happens*, she wondered as her reflection gazed back at her through the glass. Then, as if on cue, darkness started to cloud the inside like thick smoke. The ball became an inky dark mass. As she watched in wonder, a small spark of color appeared in the center and spread out, engulfing the sphere in a red orange glow. It was warm to the touch now; a comforting warmth that spread through her hands into her being.

"Fire, just like your uncle, it seems," Johnathan said, bringing her out of her trance. "A very common element, but the skill of fire is useful. That's enough for the day. You're dismissed. Pack some clothes; we'll be camping in the forest the day after tomorrow."

"Wait, wait,wait!" Mel exclaimed, jumping up and down. "Does that mean I can shoot fire beams from my eyes?"

"No."

"Breathe fire?"

"No."

"Then what's the point? Bet you can't do anything cool either." She folded her arms in a pout.

Johnathan sighed, bringing a hand up to his face. "I guess a small demonstration would be beneficial."

He held his hand out flat and small sparkles started to gleam and gather. The temperature in the room dropped slightly and a small mist formed from his breath. The sparkles gathered into a large frosty glass shard like a clear quartz crystal.

He clicked his tongue at Mel's look of skepticism. Scrunching his fingers, the shard shattered into a handful of needles. He slashed his hand down in a quick arch. The air whooshed past her as something thunked multiple times in a target board.

Mel turned on her heels, running to the board to find the needles speared through it. "That's pretty cool, actually."

"Ice has its uses," he replied as the shards melted into a fine mist with a swipe of his hand.

Mel told Daniel about the trick the next day with excited swings of her arms as they sat on a fallen log in the forest.

"My element's fire as well," Daniel said at the end of her story.

"That's all you got from that."

"No, that trick sounds pretty cool."

"Anyway. I was excited about the fire thing but then Johnathan had to ruin it by saying it's a common element," she retorted, picking at a small branch.

"It is. Heck the only time I'm dragged on a mission is to be used as a fire starter, light, and/or a pyre maker," he gripped with a small grin. "Honestly, they only want me for my fire."

"Don't be so dramatic," she bumped playfully into his side. "Being a glorified match can't be that bad. What about pyres? You mean, like a Viking funeral?"

Daniel furrowed his brows. "You could say that. How about I show you my amazing lighter abilities?"

Holding his hand out in front of Mel, Daniel ignited a small ball of fire in his palm. The bewitching flame of red and yellow tinged with blue floated eerily like a will-o'-the-wisp. He closed his hand and the flame extinguished.

"When John teaches me fire, show me how to do that!" she jumped off the log to look him straight in the eyes, transfixed in wonder.

"Wh-why? It doesn't have much use? It's just a party trick," he stammered, flushing a bright red and turning his face away.

"I could play tons of tricks on my little sister with that."

"That's mean."

"I'd apologize after." Mel gave him a sly grin as they both started laughing. "Anyway, promise you'll give me some pointers. You know, if I come back from this camping trip with John. If I'm not back in a week, consider it a lost cause, but always remember me."

Daniel laughed as small flakes of snow began to fall. "I promise, but you'll be fine. No need to be so dramatic. We should head back. It's getting cold. When it snows, it comes down fast."

A light snow filled the clearing close to the frozen stream. Johnathan had been laying out instructions on the best places to make a camp and now showing her how to inspect the area for dangers. He squatted in the middle of the space and cleared a circle of snow to reveal the cold packed earth and lined rocks around it to create a fire pit.

"Now I'll show you how to set some traps for game and collect edible plants, for winter foraging. I'll teach you how to hunt in the coming spring."

As he taught her how to build traps and pointed out plants he found a brightly colored mushroom and warned her of its dangers but also of its healing properties when used correctly. Once the temperature began to drop with the setting sun, they walked back to camp, collecting firewood and a brown hare that they had trapped.

Mel sat in front of the fire pit, striking two black stones together, sending a cascade of sparks drizzling down onto the dry branches. As soon as the sparks would land they'd instantly smolder out, filling the air with an acrid smell. Irritated, she struck the stones together in rapid succession finally making a small fire which blew out from a chilling gust. Groaning, she rummaged under a tree to grab fistfuls of dried leaves and pine needles, and then piled them onto the wood. Striking the stones again, she got a small spark that began to blaze up, eating the small offerings before catching the branches and sending inky smoke into the evening sky. She threw her head back and cackled triumphantly.

Johnathan stood over and gave her a small nod of approval. He beckoned her to follow him to the hare that lay on a flat rock; four different shaped sharp knives lay next to it. Sitting down, he proceeded to skin and gut it, instructing her how to do it as he went. Gore covered his hands up to the wrists, making Mel want to gag.

"Now when you cut the fur, make sure not to damage it too much because you can sell it later. And you can eat these bits if you'd like.

They make a nice stew." He rambled on stopping when he saw how pale she was. "Is everything all right?"

"That's utterly disgusting."

"Yes, but it'll keep you alive and fed when traveling."

"At this rate, I don't think I'll even be traveling."

"Skills need to be learned and cultivated before you can leave the village. Now if you come a little closer you can see the organs we can harvest."

"You are taking too much pleasure in this. Freak," she whispered in mock horror.

Johnathan sighed, shaking his head. "You know I had a younger brother. He'd be about your age, you remind me of him."

Mel looked up at him. "I have a little sister too! Her name's Alma. She's a bit of a scaredy cat, I wonder how her and mom are doing without me. I miss them. What's your brother like?"

Johnathan paused the knife trembling for a brief moment. His eyes appeared to cloud over as he gazed up at the dark sky and released a deep sigh. He turned back to the hare and continued cutting the meat. The silence ticked by with the crackling of the fire and Mel's stomach twisted wondering what she did wrong.

Johnathan paused again staring into the reflection of the gore smeared knife. "His name was Jackie. He was curious and followed me wherever I went. The forest was our playground. He had an odd sense of humor and was very competitive with me even though he always lost. I..." He stopped and stabbed the knife into the ground, swallowing hard. "I miss him."

"What happened to him?"

"That's in the past; let's focus on the present and dinner."

The next few days followed the same routine. Mel was glad when the experience was finally over. Sleeping in the cold on the hard pack earth was not fun or comfortable. And the way Johnathan seemed to have wiped the conversation about his brother from his mind was concerning. Most of all she hated gutting animals. She'd take the awkward silence over skinning anyday. On the last day Johnathan made her skin a small squirrel and she did a very messy job of it. She felt like a serial killer, looking at the grisly mess she made.

Training became more mundane after the little camping excursion. She'd meditated more often, hoping to develop the skill of making fire, to no avail. Her runs through the woods were not as bad anymore. Sleeping in the cold had finally acclimated her to the weather; though it didn't matter much as winter had passed, and new green life began to push through the earth to face the world.

Mel walked from the training hall, rolling her shoulders from morning stretches. She'd taken to doing them every morning even on her break days. Raised voices further ahead caused her to pause; it was odd that she didn't recognize these voices now that she'd become accustomed to most of the mansion's few residents. She continued on her way to the dining hall, hoping to avoid the now shouting voice. But as her luck would have it, the noise became louder as she got closer to her destination. From what she could tell, it was in fact only one person yelling obscenities while another seemed to be egging him on.

Walking down the stair-case, Mel came in view of the owners of the mysterious voices. Two young men stood in the entrance hall. The angry one, she presumed, was blond, pale, and dressed in dark tight clothing. The other guy had short, black hair, a jacket, and looser clothing. She quickly walked down the stairs, raising a hand to try and block her face from view, hoping to be ignored. Sadly, her attempt at discretion was in vain.

"My, my, what beautiful long hair you have. Its luster is that of obsidian," the dark-haired one literally sang.

"Oh great," was all she could grumble out. It appeared her simple and quiet day was ruined.

Chapter 12

Mel felt her hand and arm being tugged down behind her. The stranger knelt before her, clutching her hand in his. His gem-like green eyes twinkled in the torch light as he leaned forward to kiss the back of her hand, much to her disgust. Opening her mouth she was about to tell the dark haired stranger how gross that was when the blonde stomped on his head, slamming his face into the floor with a small crunch.

Mel's mouth hung open at the sheer brutality, yet her hand was still held tight. The dark-haired guy lifted his head up as if nothing happened, taking the blonde's foot and throwing it to the side. She couldn't help but feel like she was gasping like a fish at the strange display that had occurred. The stranger continued to smile at her even with his now-bleeding nose. She opened and closed her mouth a few more times, not knowing what to do or say to the strange display.

"My dear, will you tell me your name?" His green eyes still sparkled and blood dripped down his face.

"She doesn't care, you worm," the blonde growled, a storm brewing in his electric blue eyes.

"Come now, it is only right to ask someone's name, especially a beauty like her," he said with no shame, even throwing a wink for an extra measure.

Mel flushed, from embarrassment or flattery, she couldn't quite tell. She wondered if the stranger even realized his nose was bleeding. The simple fact made what would have been just an awkward flirting attempt more pathetic than anything. She tugged on her hand, trying to gently remove it from his grasp but it was no use. Giving up hope, she was about to introduce herself to the weirdo or chew her own hand off when Johnathan emerged from the dining hall and she was thankfully freed.

"John, how're you doing? How's getting old man Lupus ready for the demon council coming along?" he said, running over to him with a large grin.

Mel took her opportunity to slip by. She gave a quick wave to her teacher as he smiled back, and disappeared into the dining hall. Letting out a deep breath she didn't even know she was holding, she walked to one of the tables sitting down to eat a small breakfast. Chewing on some jerky, she thought about the two strangers. Johnathan seemed to know them. *I'll ask Daniel about them when I see him*, she thought, leaning her cheek on her fist.

While the two brushed through the horse hair from a quick ride, Mel told Daniel all about her experience that morning. He stood next to her, nodding as a small grin crept onto his face. By the end of her small story he had turned his back to her and was doubled over laughing. Squinting at him, she poked his side repeatedly.

After calming down his chuckles, Daniel flashed a wide grin at her saying, "Sounds like Dj and Spike. I knew they would be coming on business but I didn't think it would be so soon. Normally it's closer to the season's change."

"I figured you might know them," she replied, picking the wooden wire brush up again to slide it through the tan mare's mane.

"Dj really had a nose bleed the whole time?"

"Yeah, it was pretty weird how he just ignored it. I don't know if it would have been worse if he wiped his nose and pretended it didn't happen."

The two laughed at that. A warm feeling seemed to spread through her. As they walked from the stables, they chatted comfortably about how things had been going since they last spoke. Mel punched the air, pouting about still not being able to seize a win while sparring. He patted her shoulder with a small smile.

As they walked through the streets, they passed the black smith's shop where a table of metal works were out on display. Over the clanking of metal, a few of the shiny objects caught Mel's eye; in a few short steps, she was going through the table's contents, picking up and inspecting the small display of sparkling knives. One knife had a golden handle that bled into the blade giving it an elegant appearance. Another had a simple leather handle, but the blade had small swirls carved down the middle. She was so enraptured by the beauty of the blades that it didn't occur to her that Daniel had continued walking, leaving her behind. Not until she saw a knife blade that was tempered to a dark gray that was the color of his hair did she notice he was gone.

What kind of person gets so distracted by knives they forget their friend, she thought. Then again, he must not have realized they had separated either. There was no finding him at this point, so she went down one of the various alleys that webbed through the village, planning on heading back to the mansion, hoping to run into him on the way. A small smirk of pride sprung on her face at her new ability to navigate through the village. She was about to take a step back out into the bright street when a hand grabbed her elbow and spun her around.

Mel's first reaction was to throw a solid punch. A hard smack echoed in the alley-way as her assailant stopped her fist like it was nothing. Her hand stung from the impact. She glared into the stranger's green eyes, annoyed by the large smile on his handsome face.

"That's a decent punch. No need to be scared, though. I wouldn't ever hurt a girl, especially a cutie like you." He winked, releasing her hand.

Mel used all her willpower not to smash that pretty face with a kick. It was the guy from earlier, Dj, if she remembered correctly. If he was a friend of Daniel and Johnahan's it would probably look bad if she nailed him in the face. She felt a chill of disgust when he took her hand and kissed it, again.

"My name is Dj, fair lady. Now would you give me the honor of knowing yours?" he said.

Mel wanted to gag. There were only a few things that made her skin crawl; roaches, being alone in the dark, large snakes, and flirts; maybe she should add Reginald to that list. Sighing, she decided giving up would make things go more smoothly. "Melosia, but Mel is shorter and easier to remember."

"What a lovely name you have. It probably has just as sweet a meaning as it sounds. Would you care to go for tea with me?" Dj's eyes twinkled as he released her hand.

"It actually means sweet, and no thank you, I'd prefer not to," she replied, briskly walking back into the street.

"Don't be like that. I'm sure once we get to know each other it'll be fun."

"Like I already said, no thank you," she paused, turning to face him. "I'm actually looking for someone. So I'll be off."

"Your boyfriend or lover."

She spluttered, flushing, and shook her head. Thinking of Daniel like that made her head spin. "No, a friend."

"Then I don't see a problem."

Mel attempted to lose him, but Dj would not be deterred. He followed close behind, continuing to flirt and compliment her, much to her visible displeasure. He was either oblivious or just simply ig-noring the fact she was not interested in the slightest. Sure, the guy had a handsome face, nice hair, and breath-taking green eyes, but his behavior was so over-the-top. She hadn't even been interested in romance in the slightest, it just seemed like a waste of time. Just as she had reached the end of her patience, spinning upon her heel to snap at him, he skipped to a woman walking by and began to sing praises of her beauty.

Mel watched in disbelief and shook her head, thankful that he had finally left her side. As she slipped away, raised voices drifted from a tavern a few feet away. The voices were familiar and she could almost pin-point who was yelling, but she just wanted to get home at this point and opted to ignore her curiosity. Walking away, an all too familiar hand grasped her arm. She shot daggers at Dj as he held her elbow, gazing in the direction of the tavern, his eyes twinkling with mirth.

"I've made a bad first impression on you, but I think I found some-thing that might interest you," he said, a mischievous smirk playing on his face. As he dragged her into the building, she groaned in defeat.

Pipe smoke hung in the air in faint clouds. The smell of meat was strong along with stew. But what caught her attention most of all was the blonde and redhead arguing fervently in the back in front of a dartboard with multiple darts stuck in the center. It was the blonde from the morning and Reginald. They seemed close to ripping each other's throats out. It was amusing in a strange kind of way since both boys were tall and lanky, not appearing at all like either could take much of a punch. Yet, the two seemed ready to throw down right then and there.

The blonde turned his head in Mel and Dj's direction, his silver chain earrings clinging. A dark scowl spread across his face as he made his way to them, ignoring Reginald's protested squeals.

The blonde styled his shoulder length hair much like a rock star; he even had the air and presence of one. It was the polar opposite of Reginald's honor student looks.

"You're late, you wretched worm," the blonde spat, glaring at him.

"Sorry, I got a little caught up in some stuff, Spike."

"No, you didn't. You've been fooling around like the scum you are." Spike cursed, throwing a hand over his shoulder to point at Reginald. "I've had to deal with that nuisance because of it. And who are you?"

"Mel," she lifted both hands pleadingly. "I don't want to be here, this psycho stalker dragged me against my will."

"Psycho stalker, I'm hurt you think of me that way. Spike, stop glaring. You're scaring her. Remember she is special; she's old man Lupus' flesh and blood, right?" Dj said, turning to her. "I got the right girl, right?"

"Yes, you abducted the right girl. He's my uncle."

"See. She is going to be one of us, so we have to initiate her into the group."

"There is no group or initiation."

"Come on. How about this: it seems you two were at it again with the darts. How about we join in?" Dj flicked his wrist toward the dart board.

"Fine, man whore, and you scum bucket, you're going down." Spike relented, pointing first at Dj and then at Reginald.

"Are you sure about that? Is the little kitty going to show his claws?" Reginald sneered, placing his hand on his hips.

"Maybe I will, mutt."

"I don't want to be here anymore." Mel muttered turning on her heels only to be spun back around while Dj draped an arm around her shoulder, pinning her to his side.

He poked her on the nose and grinned. "Don't worry you'll get used to them in no time. I'm sure you'll make a great addition to our group."

An intense game of darts began. Mel had never played, but Dj explained that they just would see who could make the most bullseyes. It was fun and she relaxed a bit. The only problem was that Spike and Reginald were unnaturally skilled at this. Reginald's dart hit the bullseyes for the tenth time in a row making her shudder. It was terrifying how precise Reginald and Spike were at throwing darts. *I shouldn't irritate them too much*, she thought with a grimace as another dart slammed perfectly into the board.

"I see you all are having a game. Who's winning, Spike or Reginald?" Johnathan asked, walking into the tavern after some time had passed. Daniel was at his heels, a look of visible relief washing over his face when he spotted her.

Mel bounded over to the new arrivals. "I can't tell at this point. All I know is I lost and I'm scared that if I say one is winning the other might stab me repeatedly."

"I doubt they'd stab you. Throw things more like, but stabbing is definitely going too far," Daniel joked. "How badly did you do anyway? And where did you go? One second you were with me, the next you were gone."

"Actually, I didn't go anywhere. You just kept walking when I got distracted by some shiny knives, sorry. I did okay. At least I beat Dj." She gave him a sheepish grin.

"That isn't a high bar set, my dear, I for one am terrible at things that require finesse and grace." Dj shrugged before calling over his shoulder to the other two who had not stopped throwing darts. "Johnathan's here, I'm starving, let's eat and give it a rest already."

The dart duo both shot him glares that could cut like glass. Spike shoved his hands into his pockets as Reginald crossed his arms, but they walked over. The group took a seat in the corner of the tavern at a square wooden table with worn wooden benches. A few moments later a barmaid walked over to take orders.

"What lovely eyes you have, my dear. They captivate me with their beauty." Dj swooned, proceeding to heap praises onto the lady. She kindly declined his various offers.

A little after the orders were placed, the group sat and chatted about things that went right over her head she sat feeling out of place. She felt a small twine in her stomach like she was in a faraway place, observing what was happening and not sitting at the same table. She gazed down, sliding her finger along the table surface. A hand gently tapped her shoulder. Turning, she met Daniel's soft brown eyes. He smiled and nudged Dj in the side.

Dj turned to Mel. "So old man Lupus' niece right? I think I remember my dad mentioning something about him having a brother once. Supposedly he went missing."

"Yeah, well that guy winded up being my grandpa," Mel laughed, motioning with a hand. "This whole time I thought Lupus was my uncle but he's actually my great uncle. Calling him uncle though is way easier than great uncle. Less of a mouth full."

"There's a rumor that Lord Lupus got rid of his brother actually." Reginald said.

"Well, that's obviously a load of crap. You should stop listening to what old ladies gossip about and pay attention to your own life." Spike retorted, leaning back in his chair.

"If we want gossip my mom said that old man Lupus' brother left after his wife was murdered. Mom actually helped them disappear. She said it's a secret that I can't share though." Dj winked.

Spike smacked him from across the table. "Then why are you saying anything?!"

Dj winced, holding his head. "Because I thought Mel would like to know and it's in the past anyway nothing bad can come of it. It's not like Victo-," Dj released a loud yelp from multiple sharp kicks to the leg.

The silence that followed was heavy. Mel wondered what was wrong but before she could ask the server brought a platter of various items: steaming sliced meats and sausages with sage, softly baked bread, glossy with butter, a piping hot cream stew, and potatoes cubed and salted. Dj instantly started making jokes about himself and the others. Laughter replaced the odd silence that Mel had brought with her presence.

By the end of the day, Mel felt warm and happy. It had been so long since she'd hung out in a group making her feel a bit homesick for her family. She walked back to the mansion with Johnathan, a small smile on her face. She wouldn't dwell on gossip about her uncle or the rumors Reginald seemed fond of. Her uncle was odd but kind and that's all that mattered; he'd never do anything to hurt her or her family. Though she wished she knew what was so bad about his brother leaving to her world.

Chapter 13

Mel rose early the next morning, thinking of two words; demon council. Those words were mentioned many times by Dj and Spike while they conversed with Johnathan, and it appeared to be the main reason for their visit. *What is a council of demons,* she thought, pulling her hair into a bun. She'd ask Johnathan, she decided, while doing some morning stretches.

During the morning exercises, Mel struggled with the decision of when was the best time to ask Johnathan about the demon council. The indecisiveness got to the point that she was now half way through the day and she still had not found the perfect time. She wiped sweat from her forehead, leaning on her knees, trying to catch her breath in the wilderness. The smelly musk of the earth and dirt was strong today and the cicadas had started to screech at an incessant pace. It's getting warmer, she noted as the last bit of slushy snow had melted away giving rise to small sprouts and a blue dragonfly drifted past her head.

"That's it. After the run I'll do it," she vowed, believing if she said it aloud it would make her do it.

Once back in the training hall, Mel took a deep breath and strolled to her teacher, looking him dead in the eye and asked. "What's the demon council?"

Johnathan blinked a few times, bringing a thumb to his lip in thought. "It's how the tribes handle the governing of lands not under the capitals rule. Since the nobility wanted nothing to do with the ruling of this brigand and demon infested land. It's a biannual meeting held in early spring and fall. The timing varies to an extent, though."

"Will I be able to go?" She asked, leaning toward him.

"No, it's far too early for you to do anything like that." He flicked her forehead.

Scowling back at him, she rubbed her forehead. Different questions flooded through her mind. Since her uncle had elected to not say anything he deemed uninteresting during their conversation some time ago. She was curious about these things and wanted more information about the new place she called home, it was frustrating to not know anything.

"Speaking of the demon council, I think we'll end training early today. I have to make sure Lord Lupus has been doing the necessary preparations and knowing him, he probably has not. You should never speak ill of a superior, but that man is a lazy blob and the only time he uses his head is to make schemes to make me do all his work. It's hard to believe he was chosen to lead," Johnathan said, rubbing his face, a small tick appearing in his jaw.

"But can you tell me a little bit about the council?" she begged, shifting her feet from side to side.

Johnathan studied her for a moment. "There isn't much to say. Just that for a week the leaders meet to discuss various problems and ideas. Most of the time they talk circles around each other and throw insults; there is a no fighting ban during the week as well, though certain individuals find loopholes to spill blood and it isn't uncommon for people to disappear. That's the gist of it. Now I'll take my leave."

Mel was not ready for what met her the next morning. What Johnathan had said about Lupus sounded like that of a disgruntled employee, but seeing him about to throw down with her uncle this early in the morning was not what she expected when she heard bickering coming from the training hall.

Johnathan's purple locks were frizzy and an ice storm brewed in his eyes. Lupus seemed unnerved by the silent fury that radiated off the young man.

"Calm down now, Johnathan, it'll just be a day." He waved a hand nonchalantly.

"I know you well enough to know that is a lie and just an excuse. Taking Mel just solidifies my case that you are attempting to make my life harder," he snapped back, pointing a finger.

"I have to pick up some packages; if I don't they could get sold."

"You should have handled it before the eve of the council. There is planning and work to be done."

"You're always such a worry-wart. Just go with the flow. It'll keep that nice hair from turning white, though it might be a good look for you," he joked, placing a hand on Johnathan's shoulder as he seethed. He noticed his niece standing in the entrance to the room and waved her over. "Mel! I was just telling Johnathan that we will be going on a little field trip to a town outside of our borders."

"I have not agreed to this!"

"Too bad. It seems we'll be traveling with Daniel then." He grabbed Mel's arm and dragged her from the room, throwing an ineffective smoke bomb as Johnathan watched incredulously.

"Wait!"

"We'll be back later today or tomorrow. Don't worry, I'll teach her some tricks of the trade. You know how Cynthia gets when I forget her birthday." He exclaimed as they ran down the halls.

"What are we doing, Uncle?!"

"Like I said, a fun little field trip." He smiled at her as he pulled her down the stone steps, taking them three at a time. She nearly fell multiple times but her uncle's strong pull kept her from tumbling down.

They hurried to the stables where Daniel waited, leaning against the fence with three horses settled and stamping their hooves and snorting out bursts of hot air. Mel was happy to see Sandy, her favorite mare, was one of the three. She patted her snout as Lupus talked to Daniel in a quick hushed voice then, in one fluid motion, leapt onto his dark large horse, riding it in a small tight circle.

"Quickly, get on the horse," he said, glancing repeatedly in the direction of the mansion.

"We're riding through the streets?" she asked, clambering onto her mare with Daniel's help. "Isn't that rude?" she added, glancing down at Daniel who shrugged.

"No time. I don't want to take the risk that Johnathan might try to cut us off," he said, making the horse back up before sending it into a trot as the other two followed close behind. The clipping of the horse's hooves echoed through the dawn.

Lupus needn't have worried about Johnathan. As the trio crossed the small wooden bridge, all that could be seen was a couple of wolves that watched with golden eyes before slipping into the shadows after Lupus nodded at them. The bridge creaked as they passed over the gurgling stream and out of the woods into a large meadow of blooming wildflowers. The fragrance hung heavily in the air like strong perfume. The tall, dark grass that covered the field brushed against the horses' knees. Flowers in shades of red, blue, yellow, and white dotted the area, dancing lazily in the crisp warm breeze. Bird's chirped and sang. It was a beautiful and peaceful field.

"Your riding has improved," Daniel praised, pulling up close beside her.

"It's thanks to you; I would have never even given it a shot if it weren't for you." She blushed, scratching the back of her head.

"As long as we don't have to make a quick getaway we should be good," Lupus jokes.

"What is that supposed to mean?" she replied, leaning to the side in a vain attempt to grab at her uncle.

"Nothing. Now I said I'd give you some information, so here is an extra lesson with Uncle Lupus. Demons' have their own special weapons that they created themselves. These weapons have a great power and when given to a tribe member that they have partnered with, the weapon becomes a funnel to channel the demons' power."

"You can partner with demons?"

"Yup, but it's too early for that."

"Fine, tell me more about the weapons then."

"The weapons are made of a unique metal no one has yet identified . Only the demons know the true way they forge these weapons. They are insanely strong and durable, the kind of weapon that would make a blacksmith shed tears over never being able to achieve such a work of art in their lifetime. But to use their powers come with a price. It differs with each weapon. All you have to know is, the more power you use, the steeper the price," he said before trotting off ahead, sending birds and grasshoppers shying away from the grass in his wake.

"That was very informative. Wish I could know more," she muttered as Daniel chuckled at her side. They smiled and raced after Lupus through the leafy green sea of grass.

The rest of the ride was peaceful with only the occasional bird or grasshopper flying by. As they rode, the mountains became larger and seemed to bear down on the group like an ominous shadow. After leaving the meadow, it only was a small distance through a wooded area and farm land until they reached a dusty town. Its dirt roads and drab brown buildings gave it a colder feel than that of Stella Luna.

Climbing off his horse, Lupus pointed at an inn before handing Daniel a brown cloth bag that jingled. "Let's split up. I have to grab some items. You two do as you please and I'll meet you at that inn when I'm finished. Daniel, tie up the horses for us and get yourselves something to eat."

They watched as he strolled away into one of the many wooden brown and graying buildings. The duo dismounted and took the horses by the reins and walked them to the inn. It had a sign that read in yellow faded font on a dark green wooden plaque, The Wolf's Den. He passed her the reins of his horse.

"I'll go in and ask about the horses. You wait here," he said before slipping into the inn.

Mel stood to the side of the inn, gazing about while holding the horses. Sandy nuzzled the side of Mel's head while the other tapped her side with its snout, looking for treats. A small smile fell onto her face as she patted them and watched as travelers walked by. Her day had taken an interesting turn.

Chapter 14

After boarding the horses in a small barn at the edge of town, its boards turning green from age Mel and Daniel walked the streets. There were a few stores, and the odds and ends at an antique shop caught their attention for some time. They had fun playing with wooden childrens toys that Daniel talked about, reminiscing his childhood. The owner, a shrewd woman glowered at them from a distance away watching and not blinking.

Daniel bought some meat skewers dripping in berry juice for the two to share from a small food stall. They leaned against the wooden walls of a building at the end of town, watching the foot traffic that went by while eating the sweet-tasting meat. Farmers, travelers, and people selling goods came through the town taking the caravan trail leading up to the looming mountains in the distance.

Mel enjoyed these relaxed times with Daniel. She wouldn't admit it to anyone but she looked forward to seeing his bright smile after training every week, knowing that she would be teased relentlessly about it. That smile of his gave her the energy to pick herself up again after every grueling session. She cast a clandestine look in his direction, taking in his soft face, gentle brown eyes, and gray silver hair that was such a unique color. Her chest gave a small strange squeeze as she looked down at her dust covered black boots kicking the dirt around.

The sun rose high into the sky and had just begun its descent casting dark shadows across the ground. Lupus had not appeared yet at the meeting point. They agreed to go inside the Wolf's Den just in case he had already entered and they had not noticed.

The Wolf's Den had two floors and a wide open floor plan. The beams that supported the roof were painted a dark green. There was a small eating area with tables placed in the entry in front of rows of dark green doors in the back. A large staircase leads to the open ledge of the second floor.

"Evening. Has a man named Lupus come inside?" Daniel asked the owner, a stout man with silvering hair.

"Yes, he came in earlier to rent a room. Do you want the key?" he asked, disappearing under the desk and reappearing with an old rust colored skeleton key.

Daniel nodded, releasing a long sigh, taking the key and asked. "Which room?"

"Second floor, room 19."

Daniel gave a small thanks then led Mel to the room. The second floor's doors were the same green with dark knobs. The room had three small beds and a tiny table in the back. Rubbing his forehead, Daniel collapsed onto one of the beds.

"John's going to be ticked."

"I'm going out on a limb here but from the room and his MIA status, I think Uncle plans on staying the night, right?" Mel jokes, taking a seat with a bounce next to him.

"That is correct," Lupus exclaimed, seeming to have magically materialized.

Daniel gave a small strangled yelp and fell off the bed with a thump, wide-eyed. Mel looked down at him. He panted as he blinked. She placed a hand on his head, and tousled his soft locks. He gave her a sheepish grin.

"Sorry," he muttered, flushed as he took his spot on the bed next to her again a little further away.

She shook her head, waving off his apology. Turning to her uncle, she had to be frank with him. "You promised Johnathan we'd be back tonight. The ride didn't take that long to get here."

"It's evening now. We'd be riding in the dark, and John is used to this kind of behavior by this point. Let's relax for the time being, alright?" He said with a small smile. He then pulled a leather book from his bag. "Would you look at this; it's a book on children's fables," he added, tossing it to his niece. She scrambled to catch it.

"It's not much of a bribe, but I don't know how to get back and being alone in the woods is..." She trailed off, waving the book to the side, trying to pick out the right words.

"Scary, terrifying, and or lonely." Daniel listed off his fingers.

Mel shoved him with her shoulder. In retaliation, he snatched the book and stood up, keeping it out of her reach. Lupus watched as the two scrambled around the room.

Mel hadn't realized she had fallen asleep, but the soft light of the sun streaming in from the window was a good indicator that she had. Sitting up and stretching, she yawned, then rubbed her eyes. Blinking the sleep from her eyes, she noticed something very wrong. The two other beds were empty with the sheets spread tight as if nobody had slept in them. Jumping up, she looked around the room, noticing that their bags were also gone. She rocked on her heels feeling unease as she scanned the room. Then her eyes landed on a note pinned to the door. She pulled the faded paper with a sharp tug.

"Morning, Melosia, this is your uncle. I bet you are wondering where we are. We left you in the night; a sleep and dash, you might say. This is a test, to see if you can make it back on your own. Simple right? P.S. I didn't pay for the room and this inn is notorious for punishing patrons that don't or can't pay. So it's best to sneak out. I'd personally escape from the window." She stared at the paper, then read through it again to make sure she read it correctly.

"What the heck, is a sleep and dash?!" she asked the emptiness in disbelief, crushing the note and then tossing it at the wall. "I hate my Uncle. What's with this childish prank?!"

Sighing, she opened up the window, then stuck her head out. There were some dark vines growing down the building. She popped her head back in. Jumping on the balls of her feet, she attempted to psych herself up. Then she took a deep breath and let it out slowly. *This is illegal on so many levels*, she thought, grimacing, as she attempted to scale the building. Her first few moves went well. The tick vines seemed to support her. But then her foot slipped and she crashed painfully on her back. Stars flashed before her eyes; her head swirled making it difficult to breathe for a few seconds. She rolled onto her feet and ran through the village in what she hoped was the right direction.

She was passing through a farm when she heard a commotion. Raised voices jeering and cursing. She glanced to her right where the noise came from and saw four teen boys holding shovels and rakes. They were gesturing at a tiny lump in the middle of their circle. Mel was going to ignore it but then she heard a meow. Her head whipped around, her eyes meeting the sad pleading golden eyes of a small kitten. It squeaked wheezily, almost sounding like it was begging for help.

Mel set her jaw as the kitten meowed again causing her to spin on her toes and run at the group, and flung herself in front of the kitten.

"What do you think you're doing?" One of the boys spat, leaning on his rake as he glared with dark eyes.

"I should be asking you that. What kind of sick person gets fun out of abusing animals?" she snapped, returning his glare.

"It's all just fun, and anyway, it's better if we kill it now while it's small. Get out of the way."

"No."

They stared each other down. The seconds ticked by. The tension was as tight as a spring.

The kitten tried to flee, and one of the guys made a move to grab it, but Mel scooped it up with her left hand, ducking under a punch. She spun to the side, trying to get distance. She easily slid out of the way of the blows thrown her way. She bobbed and weaved, not wanting to fight back. A small spark of confidence filled her as she spun out of the way of the rake. She smirked. This was nothing compared to the hell of training with the others. This was easy mode.

A shovel smashed into the side of her head, causing her to stagger. She stumbled to the side as the world seemed to totter. Her head throbbed in pain as her vision sparked. Something dripped into her eye. She wiped it away to see blood. Her vision fizzled at the sight making her knees weak. When she saw the brown haired boy lift up his rake to smack her. Rage filled her like a tidal way. She had not suffered through getting beaten by Johnathan to get hurt by a couple of jerks.

Mel caught the rake before it hit her and slammed her foot into the boy's gut, and sent him reeling as she wrenched the rake from him. She spun the rake around and used it to sweep the feet out from under the one with the shovel. Using the rake as leverage, she pole vaulted herself up and slammed her boot into another's face with a small crunch. Landing, she drove her elbow into the side of the final boy.

"Still want to go?" she snarled, throwing her head back.

The boys looked at each other and then ran away. She ran a few paces behind them, waving the rake. "Come back and face me cowards!"

Grumbling, she tossed the rake and continued on, wiping her head every so often and swaying. Once she made it to the woodland, she sat down and leaned against a birch tree. The kitten meowed as she placed it down. Her head was swimming and the adrenaline was gone, leaving her feeling nauseated. The splitting pain in her head made her close her eyes and she drifted off.

A rough tongue scratched against Mel's cheek, stirring her. Raising back up, she cradled her throbbing head. Her mouth felt like cotton. A small body rubbed against her boots and meowed, its fur covered in dirt and grim.

"You stayed with me to see if I was okay, let me check you out, too. It's only fair," she said, picking up the kitten and walking to a small creek. She dunked the kitten into the crisp water and to her surprise, was met with little resistance. On inspection, the kitten seemed to be in great health. Its brown fur was spotted and thick but there were no wounds to be found.

"I don't want to leave you, but you look like a wild cat, and your parents are probably near. We're far enough from those mean guys, they shouldn't hurt you now," Mel said, scratching the little kitten behind its ears. It purred in reply.

Mel smiled and shared what little food she had. Standing up, the kitten ran into the trees and waited, watching.

"What is it? Do you live here? I have to go now. By then," she said. The kitten turned its head away and seemed to slump.

It didn't feel quite right to leave the kitten, but it seemed content enough to stay in the woods. Mel smiled, waving to the little guy and headed toward the flower meadow. As she walked, the hair on the back of her neck stood up. Something was very wrong, but she couldn't put her finger on what it was. As she walked through the thick, waist-length grass, everything appeared the same as the day before. The only difference was that there was no sound. The birds and insects were eerily silent. A chill ran up her spine and she involuntarily shivered in the warm breeze.

She gulped and sprinted through the field, not caring if she appeared foolish. Her whole being told her to get away. The grass scratched at her legs and she tripped on a gopher hole but rolled back onto her feet in an instant. She had to get to the woods but the bridge was too far. The primal terror propelled her. She leapt over the stream, just making it to the opposite side, pin wheeling her arms to keep balance. When she reached the woods, a wall of sound rushed in around her from all sides, but she didn't care, she had to keep running.

As the girl's back disappeared into the thick wilderness; death slithered into the meadow. Nature seemed to be holding its breath as the large beast hissed eerily, its dark green scales gleaming in the light. The snake raised its massive head in the direction of the mountain's cloudy peaks. Its yellow slanted eyes blinked. A large forked tongue flicked out, tasting the air. A sinister smile, if you could call it that, stretched across its face as it slithered toward its new destination, leaving a trench of uprooted dirt in its wake. In the distance, the wolves howled.

Chapter 15

Mel ignored the questioning looks she received walking down the streets of Stella Luna. All she wanted was a hot bath and rest. Any pride she felt of finding her way home was hidden behind the woozy exhaustion she felt. Thankfully, no one she knew saw her in this disheveled state, of dirt and dried blood staining the side of her head. Climbing up the stone stairs was a chore, and when she arrived in her room, she collapsed onto her bed, letting the soft sheets envelop her. Blinking, with her head still throbbing, she fought to keep her eyes open but in seconds her eyes rolled back and she was out.

Being violently shaken woke Mel from her stupor. She stared groggily at her uncle, mind blurry and mouth dry. His forehead was creased with worry. She slurred a few words before her head lulled backward. A small snore escaped her lips, causing Lupus to snort.

Mel's eyes shot open as she lunged from her bed, yelling, "I'm late for school!"

"Wait, no. What time is it?" She rubbed her face, feeling a soft bandage on her temple and a small note that had not been there before.

She changed her clothes and washed the grime off her face before walking to the dining hall, hoping she hadn't slept past dinner. In the dining hall, the smell of baked meat and bread hung heavy in the air. She spotted her uncle surrounded by Johnathan, Reginald, and Tsume. Striding over she took a seat.

"Sleeping Beauty has finally joined us," Lupus exclaimed, stretching his arms out.

"What happened to you?" Tsume asked, touching the bandage on Mel's head.

Mel flinched at the small tingle of pain. "Nothing. I tripped in the forest and smacked my head on a tree stump." She shot a venomous look at Reginald when he snickered.

"Can we get back to business?" Johnathan asked, tapping a long finger on the table. "Tsume, where's your husband?"

"With the kids. They've got a cold," she replied, taking a snip from her silver goblet.

"Wait, wait, wait, hold on a second. How long was I asleep? Did I have a concussion and slip into a coma? I knew you were married but when did you have kids?!" Mel jumped up, fully awake. The action made her light headed. Her vision swam.

Tsume threw her head back, laughing with a large grin. "Since before you came here. You totally thought they were my mom's kids didn't you!"

Mel turned to the side, crossing her arms. "No, that would be dumb."

"Yes you did! Admit it!" Tsume said, throwing the poor girl into a headlock.

"Never!"

"Getting on to more important matters," Johnathan said, ignoring the two. "The demon council is in a few days. We are here to give out the assignments. Tsume, you and Kiba will stay in charge of the village and handle Mel's training between yourselves. Lupus, Reginald, Daniel, and I will be going to the meeting." He listed out different jobs and boring details for the next week making Mel's mind drift off and, judging from Tsume's glazed look, she wasn't the only one.

"We leave tomorrow morning," Lupus said, examining his nails, bringing the meeting to a blissful end. "You are dismissed."

Despite Johnathan's best attempts, the next morning's departure was not a smooth affair. Lupus' unfinished essential documents seemed to be the last straw. Johnathan slammed a thick pile of papers into Tsume's hands and furiously dragged the group out of the mansion fuming; giving only a curt nod of goodbye.

"That was a scene. An expected one, but still a scene." Tsume giggled, smacking her husband on the back.

"Hello, I've been on assignments the last few months and never gotten the proper opportunity to introduce myself after our first interaction, I'm Kiba." He smiled kindly, extending his hand.

"We don't have time for that. It's time to train. I promise I'll be a lot more fun than that stick in the mud Johnathan." Tsume exclaimed, punching the air.

"Tsume, please calm down."

"I am calm. I'm always calm; now let's get pumped!"

Mel sat on the cold floor of the training hall, watching as the other two read through the instructions Johnathan had given them. After they'd finished a sheet, they would trade like clockwork. It was strange how in sync they were.

"Your training will be relatively the same as it has been, except Lady Cornelia will be helping now in the morning to nurture your element. We will also start going over different weapons and fighting styles that might suit you," Kiba explained, pacing. "Tsume, do you think you can handle it and not go overboard?"

"I never go overboard, love," she replied, draping an arm around him and kissing his temple.

"I'll help with weapon sparring but that's it. If you need me, I'll be purging Lord Lupus' office, excuse me, organizing it. Evidently, things got hectic." He sighed, slinking off with a slouch.

"Are you ready to die," Tsume exclaimed, "of fun?!"

"I guess?"

"I hope so, children," a voice announced as Lady Cornelia entered the room, her hair flowing behind her like a cloak. "Here you go," she added, giving Mel a parcel.

"Thanks. What is it?"

"A dress like mine. I hope it fits. Go try it on," Cornelia said, pointing to a closet door.

Mel stepped into the dark closet and a candle blazed to life showing the small confines. She pulled out the silk dance outfit, its scarlet fabric glittering like fire in the torch light. Sighing, she struggled to pull it on, stepping on the skirt and falling over, hitting the wall with a painful thunk. The top was longer than Cornelia's and the colors differed. She felt foolish wearing something so showy as she exited the room, holding her hands in front of the small bit of her stomach that showed.

"It fits, but why did you give me..." She trailed off, not knowing how to phrase the question and not come off rude or ungrateful.

Another door opened and Tsume spun out, wearing an identical dress in silver and light blue, exclaiming with a flourish. "We match!"

"It's simple. One of the best ways to train in the arts is to dance for the spirits of the elements. It pleases them and makes them more accommodating to our wishes," Cornelia said, waving her arms. "You will follow my movements and learn the dances of the elementals."

The week went by with relative ease. Cornelia, Tsume, and Mel would dance every morning. At first it was awkward, but as the days passed they moved in unison. Mel discovered she had a knack for dancing. She took to the dances with glee. Her favorites were the fire and wind dances for the speed and flowing grace they shared. After every dance, she was sat down and given a candle to light. She'd sit and stare, concentration creasing her brows but the candle would not light. Towards the final days a small line of smoke would appear for a second, but no more.

After dancing, she'd run through the woods. Yet now when she passed the meadow, her stomach would turn with unease. She felt foolish for the paranoia that bubbled inside her.

Sparring was a different matter altogether. Kiba trained her with a different weapon each day. First, it was small blunt knives, spears, staffs, swords, and then bows. Mel enjoyed the swords best. She was clumsy with the long staff and spear, and getting too close to her opponent with knives made her uncomfortable. Swords allowed her to fight at the perfect distance, she felt. She enjoyed these matches though she could see a calculating look in Kiba's blue eyes as if he was grading her constantly.

The problem arose when it was Tsume's time to spar.

The hand to hand with Tsume would start off simple, but then she'd get too excited. In one session, her powerful punch to Mel's gut sent Mel sprawling and skidding halfway across the floor. Mel dry heaved, coughing violently, covering her mouth, to try and stifle the coughs she felt something wet and sticky coat her hand. She paled, feeling her stomach plummet when she glanced down at her hand and saw red sticky blood splattered on it. The room began to spin as her ears rang. She collapsed backward. Her only thoughts were she must be dead.

Mel woke, coughing in the infirmary, a disgusting metallic taste coating the inside of her mouth. She turned her head and her eyes met those of the twins. The girls had short brown hair, golden eyes, and tanned skin. They smiled in unison, cocked their heads to the side.

"She's up," they exclaimed, running over to Storm who seemed to be in a deep discussion with Tsume.

Tsume looked like a beaten puppy caught doing something bad. The usual prideful tilt of her head was replaced with a down-cast gaze and slumped shoulders.

"You should be glad you didn't break any of her bones, or cause any intense internal damage. Honestly, I raised you better than this," Storm chided before kneeling and patting the girls on the head. "My little assistants are doing well. How did you give birth to such angels?" she added, cooing.

"Mom, stop! She's up. I want to get back to training. I want to rub it in John's face that I'm the better teacher. I love bugging that boy," she whined, balling her fists.

"No more training for today or tomorrow. She is going to take it easy after the number you did on her this week. Also she hit her head when she fell. She isn't prepared for damage like that yet," she stated, walking over to give Mel a bowl of green liquid. "Drink," she commanded, gently patting her head.

Mel scrunched up her nose at the pungent smell. Brining it to her lips, she almost drank, but the stench made her turn her head away. Then, seeing Strom's expectant gaze, she swallowed it in one go, gagging at the chunks that slid down her throat. She lay back down, and Storm pulled the covers over her with a sweet smile.

"This week has been rough on you. Just rest for now," she said, walking past her daughter with a reprimanding glance.

"I guess that's that. Kiba made a small list of what strategies he thinks will work for you, given Johnathan's plans. Look over it with your new free time." Tsume glumly gave her the papers, then got dragged by her small girls. She paused, calling out, "But there are no problems you can't solve with just your fists and the element of surprise."

After glancing through the small list, Mel came to a conclusion. Kiba was good at making detailed observations. His notes were in depth. It appeared Mel lacked power and stamina, no surprise there, she snorted, then clenched her stomach as pain shot through her, but flexibility and speed were her high points. *I can fix those weak points easily*, she thought. She drifted off imagining being a ninja like her favorite character from Knights of the Night, Nina the betrayed assassin.

Chapter 16

When the others returned from the council, they had two extras in tow in the forms of Dj and Spike. The group had gone to the tavern again to eat and were talking about how the week went on both sides. Johnathan had his head in his hands as Mel spoke.

"I knew Tsume was tough but I didn't think a punch could feel like getting hit by a truck." She finished her story while flailing her arms about.

"What's a truck?" Dj asked.

"A big vehicle that goes vroom vroom," she replied, making more hand motions. "A kind of carriage from where I'm from," she added at the confused looks she received and dropped it when she saw the dark look Johnathan shot her way. .

"Well, nothing of interest happened on our end. Just the same old boring politics. Thieves are raiding this area and a demon was close to our borders. Your tribe's problems don't matter, ours are more important," Dj said, pitching his voice to a whining tone and raising a hand.

"You're forgetting how you almost got gutted for flirting with a man's wife." Spike smirked.

"Let's not remember that part," Dj sighed.

Reginald took a sip of tea before speaking. "Johnathan, as always, was the definition of respectable. Unlike other people."

"Reg, we're trying to be friendly, not start fights," Daniel said, waving his hands.

"I'm sorry for speaking the truth."

"Did she actually knock you out? We'll have to put endurance and pain tolerance on your training now, it seems," Johnathan said after much thought, ignoring the bickering that was going on around them.

"Please don't."

"Oh, and we should start on other tolerances as well, like poison, and probably work on your stealth," he continued, oblivious to Mel's objections.

Spike snorted, crossing his thin arms. "There's no point in stopping him when he gets like that. He's going to do whatever the hell he wants. It's how he's always operated."

"I feel sorry for you already, my love. Try not to eat anything he offers," Dj said.

"Good luck. You're going to need it." Spike placed a hand on her shoulder with a smirk.

The next day went like normal with only small additions. Exercise, dance, meditation, running, sparring, and a lecture. Mel beamed when the candle she needed to light started to smolder. The acrid fumes gave rise to hope that fire was near.

"You'll be able to start and have basic control of fire soon," Johnathan noted with a small smile and hint of pride in his voice. "Now, Kiba gave me the data he collected. Have you thought it over?"

"Yes, I would prefer to use a sword and I want to focus on speed and power; I'll be like a ninja or an assassin," she punched the air with vigor. "If you don't mind, would you tell me how you fight?"

"I use swords as well," he replied with a small nod. "That's a good process to start, but I'll have you learn all the weapons to get the basics. It's never a bad thing to be prepared for any problem."

Looking down at her dirt covered shoes, she bit her lip and shifted her weight back and forth. Taking a small breath, she proceeded to ask about something that had interested her. "Johnathan, can you give me some information about demons? Whenever I ask uncle, he dances around the subject and you seem to ignore it as well. It's just kind of odd since they're important and dangerous here, and when I went with uncle, he mentioned something about partnerships with them."

He stared at her for what felt like an eternity. She wondered if she should retract the request as the time silently ticked by. Wringing her hands together, she was about to speak when Johnathan groaned loudly, clutching his head in his hands.

"Are you telling me Lord Lupus told you the bare minimum?" he asked, and she gave him a small nod. "This whole time I assumed that he had said more, but I guess he just left it for me to do like everything else." He signaled her to sit as he paced with his arms folded behind his back.

"I'll do a crash course through demon relations with the tribes. There are two types of partnerships. Summoning allows you to use the demon's power through their weapon for a certain price. Normally it's called a blood price but blood is rarely required. It depends on the demon. The other type of partnership is a bonded demon that stays by your side. Both have benefits and draw-backs. A bonded demon is always with you, meaning you have a partner, but you can't funnel their power for yourself. With a summoning, you can use their power at will, but the price is steep. With bonding, the demon can be hard to control."

"Now, with summoning, every tribe has one exceedingly strong summoning. That would be the patron or guardian demon and you have to be contracted with them to be considered the leader of your tribe. Ours is named Iceshera, she is bonded to Lord Lupus. Sometimes a tribe may have two patron's if another tribe gifted it to them. We have a secondary patron that another tribe could not handle."

"Now, there is a saying told to young children to not help an animal in need because you never know if it is a demon in disguise. Demons are many things, but they do pay off their debts. They can do it by contracting with you or helping you out, and when I say helping, it's normally not in a good way. An example would be a demon pushes you off a cliff to stop you from tripping on a rock. It's hard to trust a demon at your side because you never know if they will try to kill you by being helpful."

"That was a very unique example. Did you get pushed off a cli…" The words died in Mel's throat at the dark glare she received.

"Anyway, it is best to use caution in these matters. Now, I'm going to have a surprise for you at breakfast." He grinned, clapping his hands together.

Mel lay crumpled on the floor in agony, coughing up phlegm, shaking violently. She wished she remembered Dj's warnings days before. A small jar of bright yellow liquid was placed in front of her. Looking up took almost all her strength; her vision was spotty and she thought she might pass out. Johnathan smiled sympathetically at her.

"I'd drink it, if I were you," he said and she swallowed the sickeningly sweet liquid.

The pain in her body receded slowly, replaced by a tingle from her center that spread to her fingers. Leaning on her tingling hands, she glared up at him, not even having the strength to shoot accusations at him.

"I poisoned your meal. It'll be like this for the next few weeks until you gain a resistance to most poison." His smile did not match the sinister sentence. "Chin up, that was the weakest that I could whip up on short notice."

Mel would have screamed if her throat didn't feel so swollen. She thought they had become friends and he pulled this crap on her. This was betrayal. If this was just the beginner level of poison, then the next few weeks were not going to be fun. She grimaced, cradling her cloudy head in her still shaky hands.

It was a living hell. Fast acting powerful poisons were constantly placed into her meals. Even when she tried to outsmart Johnathan, he would still get her to consume the toxins one way or another. He was crafty and sly, always two steps ahead. The antidotes were close by, but that didn't make the fact she was being poisoned on a daily basis any better.

Salvation came when Johnathan told her that she had now a passable resistance to the most common poisons. They were the words of an angel from the mouth of a devil. He then added that if she were poisoned, she'd probably just get unbearably queasy.

Just because she was being poisoned didn't mean Johnathan relented in his barbaric training. He actually made it worse, adding weapon drills. She had to swing a heavy practice sword until her arms ached and felt like they would fall off. Her elbows creaked and cracked by the end of those long training sessions. He continued to have her use other tools as well, having her shoot multiple arrows a day till her fingers were cut and calloused.

"Johnathan, when can I go on a mission?" she asked, laying on her now best friend; the ground. It was the first blessed day of being free of the poison.

"It's too soon for that."

"Too soon! It's almost summer. Come on, I can fight now, defend myself. Let me shadow a mission, please," she begged, attempting to stare him down.

"Maybe when you can summon a fire; I could use you as a fire starter," he joked, shrugging.

Mel scowled. Even after so much time meditating, dancing, and staring at the dang candle it would not light, only smoke. She sat up, lifting her chin, and squinted at him before speaking. "Fine, when I summon fire; you'll take me on a mission."

"Maybe. We'll see."

"Promise me that you'll do it. Swear it!" she demanded, waving her arms with all the menace of a small dog.

"Fine, but with how it's been going, you won't be going on a mission until winter," he teased, poking her forehead. "But if you can't even win one duel with Reginald, I don't think it'll be even that soon," he added as the red head appeared.

"You think you can beat me princess?" Reginald said, swinging the practice sword.

"You bet, Chupacabra."

The two dove, swinging the swords in swift succession. They parried and lunged in a dance of wooden blades, vying for the upper hand. Crossing the swords, they came to a blade lock then jumped back to separate.

Mel glowered, panting. She was going to win this duel no matter what. An idea sprang in her head, remembering something Tsume had told her about surprises and fists and since Johnathan wasn't watching it was the perfect time. She charged ahead, throwing the practice sword at the redhead. He batted the sword away, confused. That small distraction was all she needed. Pulling back her arm, Mel smashed her fist into his face using the velocity of her run to increase the power. Reginald crumpled backward, rolling onto the floor yelling and clutching his face.

Jumping in glee, Mel let out a roar of victory. "I win!"

"Yeah. One out of what, fifty or so losses?"

"It doesn't matter, loser, I win this competition!"

"It was a cheap shot!"

"Sounds like something a loser would say."

"I want a rematch."

"Sorry. I have to rest for tomorrow. Noche," she replied sweetly, dashing away.

Chapter 17

Mel crouched in the underbrush, the leaves scratching against her cheek. She watched the young buck graze. Holding the bow shakily in her hands and strung an arrow; pulling the feathered end back. Taking aim, she held her breath. The wind changed. The deer's ears became alert and it swung its head in her direction, staring with brown eyes. She panicked, releasing the arrow that whizzed harmlessly over the buck's head as he dashed away.

She groaned, taking a few steps to the tree in which the arrow was embedded and ripping the shaft out. With a lowered head, Mel trudged back to the small camp that Johnathan and she had made.

"I almost had a deer," she muttered, placing the bow down.

"It's fine. We can catch some fish. You can try again to hunt tomorrow."

Mel started stacking firewood. Then she stared at the pile, willing it to burn but only some smoke rose.

"Just use the fire starter," Johnathan said, walking toward the stream.

With the end of spring, deer had come to the forest that surrounded Stella Luna, and Johnathan thought it would be an excellent chance to teach her to hunt. There was one goal for this outing: for Mel to kill a deer. She had been at it for three days at this point. They would spar, hunt, and then spar again. That's how the days had gone. If any more days passed she worried that others might think Johnathan had finally killed her and disposed of her body.

What was so great about killing a deer? She could catch rabbits and fish, and she could butcher them decently, even if she did find the process revolting. But when she brought these points up, Johnathan seemed adamant that she learn to hunt bigger game.

"You can get more meat from a deer and the fur can be used for more things as well," Johnathan retorted when she brought the subject up again on her fifth failure.

"If anything, this excursion should prove I'm ready to go on a mission. Forget the deer," she whined as she scaled a small silver fish.

Johnathan put down the branch he was carving to walk toward her. "You can't even make a fire without a fire starter, your stealth is lacking, and you don't know how to tend a wound."

"Do those things really matter? You have to use a fire starter."

He placed a hand on her head. "Melosia, you have a knack for sneaking around. Don't make a face, I've noticed you do. You would be an excellent hunter if you would just polish your skills. That is what this hunting lesson is for."

"Fine. But you haven't even gone over wound-tending yet."

He was silent for a few moments, thinking, then a small smile and twinkle flashed in his eyes. "You are right. Maybe it's time you learned."

"Great. How will we do it? What will we practice on?" she asked, excited for something different from the old schedule; missing the small and dangerous glint in his eyes.

"You," he stated simply, still smiling.

"What?" She cocked her head to the side, wrinkling her forehead.

"You," he repeated.

With a flash Johnathan, slashed her left arm with his small knife. She stared in shock and horror as a small red line appeared and blood began to bubble and pour down her arm. She stared at him, wide-eyed, mouth agape.

"Now, all you have to do when you don't have the necessary materials is cut some cloth from your clothing," Johnathan explained as if he hadn't just cut her.

Finally finding her voice, she shrieked, "Estas loco? What is wrong with you?!" Pain ran up her arm and blood ran down in crimson rivulets, making her light headed.

"No," he replied, appearing genuinely confused.

"You can't just stab someone! That hurt you, psycho! Tu es loco!" she yelled, trailing off into a tirade of Spanish insults. She fumbled with bloodied fingers through her bags, looking for bandages and began wrapping her arm, using her teeth to pull the white cotton tight. The fabric was smeared with blood from her shaking hand.

"You should clean the injury first with water."

Mel just stared at him, maintaining eye contact, as she ignored his instruction and continued to wrap her arm. Then she picked up the fish that was half cleaned and threw it at him. Grabbing her bow she made a rude gesture at him and attempted to leave but was stopped by a strong grip on her arm.

"Stop being a brat!" He silenced her by yanking the hasty bandages off and forcing her to sit.

They sat in a fuming silence as Johnathan tended to the cut. He paused, sighing, "Remember how I told you about my little brother? He died because of me...my whole family died in less than a week because of me. I was impulsive, prideful, and weak and because of me they all are gone. Jackie, bleeding out on my back, and my mother's cold hand. Those feelings will haunt me for the rest of my life and the thought that if I was only stronger they'd still be here. If I wasn't a weak child my family would be safe."

Mel listened. The tremble in Johnathan's voice cast away her anger as he paused from wrapping her arm to look at the sky to calm himself. What he said reminded her why she was here, to protect her mother and sister. The thought occurred to her of what life would be like if all her family was gone, it made her stomach turn.

"That's why I'm so hard on you and my other failed students. A life can end in only a moment. I don't want to lose anyone else I care for," he said, placing a gentle hand on her head giving her a tender smile. "Even a bratty younger sibling."

Johnathan rose walking back to the fire as Mel sat mulling over his words. She picked her bow back up calling to him, "I am Melosia, fighter of bullies, student of Johnathan, and soon to be bane of deer. First of my name!"

He watched, raising an eyebrow as she turned and ran into the woods. He brought a hand to his mouth to stifle a small laugh at her antics to cheer him up.

The sound of rustling bushes woke Mel. The forest was full of thick morning fog. She pushed off the tree she slept on, winching as pain shot through her cut arm. The rustling came from her right. She strung the bow, feeling the taut string under her fingers. She gritted her teeth, swinging the bow around toward the sound. Nothing. She crouched, then moved closer to the sound, balancing on the balls of her feet to muffle the sound. In a small clearing, a deer stood. The sun's rays cut through the fog like spotlights. In one swift silent movement, she pulled back the bow and released the arrow. The deer staggered as he was pierced through the throat, then took a few steps before collapsing.

Mel released her breath and dropped her tense shoulders. Unhanding the bow, she collapsed to her knees, pumping her fists into the air with a giddy grin. She grabbed one of the deer's antlers, and began dragging the deer back to camp with a small feeling of pride and lingering sadness for the majestic creature's short life.

Up to his elbows in blood, Johnathan happily told Mel of all the different uses for the meats, organs, bones, and hide of a deer. He seemed creepily cheery as he wiped his forehead, smearing blood absentmindedly. He offered her the knife to help with the cleaning. Her stomach turned at the prospect of touching the disgusting heap of flesh, but she took the knife, not wanting him to stab her again.

Later, Mel sat in front of the fire pit, smacking the stones together with no avail. She was irritable. Her arm hurt and they were going to stay out here for another day. Throwing the smooth black stones at a tree, she growled and cursed the fire pit. The smell of smoke filled the air followed by a whoosh as the pit erupted in a blazing torrent that dwindled into a small flame. Her face was hot from the heat, she turned to Johnathan, a small smirk was on his lips as he raised an eyebrow.

"Congrats. You can now be used as a fire starter it seems."

Mel glanced at the small dancing flames and jumped up and down yelling. "I did it! I did it! Take that, nature! Not only can I hunt, but I can make fire as well! Take that!"

Johnathan stifled a laugh at her glee. "I guess this means we can head back to the village in the morning, and you can go on the next mission. A promise is a promise."

On the way back to the village they left most of the deer at one of the farms and the family was quite happy with the gift. The villagers, in turn, gave them a basket full of vegetables and said they would continue to pray to the spirits for Lord Lupus' good health.

Three days later, Johnathan informed Mel of a mission they would be going on the next day and instructed her to prepare. "Go let Storm take your measurements for a proper outfit."

Mel nodded, then sprinted to the other side of the mansion before he could change his mind.

"What do you want? Any preferences?" Tsume asked Mel as her mother jotted down the measurements.

Mel cocked her head. Thinking about it, she always imagined having a cool outfit. But cool wasn't practical. A full suit of sparkling armor would boil her alive in the warm air. Skimpy clothes would just be ridiculous. Imagine telling your ancestors you died in a sword fight while wearing a bikini. She chuckled to herself. Cool will kill you, practical will keep you alive.

"Storm, make whatever you think is practical." She paused as an idea hit her. "But I would like a hood."

"Alright, dear, I'll leave it for you at your door in the morning." Storm smiled, scribbling away on her notepad.

Mel stopped on her way out, a thought causing her to flush. Exhaling from her nose, she turned shyly and scratched her head. "Actually, if it isn't too much trouble, an outfit similar to Johnathan's would be good."

"I understand." Storm smiled again as Tsume hid her cheeky grin behind her sleeve.

Mel rose early and blurry eyed, but was wide awake in moments at the thought of her first adventure. She found the package for her outfit next to her door just like Storm had promised.

Looking herself over in the mirror, Mel noticed the small changes her body had gone through over the past months. She was thinner, leaner, and her hair had grown longer. The outfit was black and brown with an undershirt and shorts. A short hooded vest with a large star and moon embroidered in red on the back. Her favorite part was the red-trimmed half skirt that was attached to the shorts. Glancing in the mirror again she thought she resembled a thief.

She walked proudly with her head high to the entrance hall. Tsume and Johnathan were waiting. Johnathan wore dark clothes as well as a blue skirt tail much like her own with two long sabers strapped to his waist.

"Awww, you two match," Tsume teased, covering her grin with her large embroidered sleeves.

"That outfit suits you," Johnathan said, pulling a long parcel from his back and handing it to her. "A gift for your hard work."

Mel took the package with great care, feeling a small warmth in her chest. Unwrapping the soft cloth revealed the gleam of a saber. Its hilt was made of soft leather with a small blue tassel dangling from the end. She cradled the sword to her chest, her eyes misting up. "Thank you, I love it."

The trio then made their way from the village to the small town near the mountain chain. They were riding their horses through the meadow when Johnathan began to explain the mission that was given to them.

"Many of the merchants that supply our village with goods have been going missing along the trail through the mountain chain for over a couple of months now. We are going to investigate and find out what is happening to them."

"Then we crush the problem to dust," Tsume said, clenching her fist.

"As I was saying," Johnathan shot her a warning look. "We will head up the mountain after asking around town if anyone has noticed anything strange."

Mel sat with the horses as the other two walked around the town. Leaning against a fence she sighed, sliding down. Babysitting horses was not what she had expected to do on her first real adventure. A dark brown horse chewed on her ponytail. She pushed the horse's snout away ignoring its nicker. Movement in the shadows caught her eye. She walked over to the alley, but saw nothing. She shook her head, deciding lack of sleep made her see moving shadows. She yawned as her partners returned.

The horses were left behind as the group began their hike to the mountains that loomed ahead after learning many travelers had also recently gone missing. It wasn't that long of a walk, but Mel's feet hurt by the time they made it to the foot of the mountain. A bead of sweat rolled down her neck as she gazed up at the mountain's dark mass. Taking a deep breath, she steeled herself for a long, hard hike.

The hike was hard. And hot. The path that they followed was well trodden, and the packed, rocky earth wasn't the best on the ankles. The thick, green vegetation seemed to be closing in around the path. Vines, trees, bushes, and clumps of flowers were all one could see in the sloping land. The cicadas buzzed, birds sang, and every now and then, an animal would dart by. A deer, squirrels, even foxes, scurried out of view.

After stopping for a small break, they were now half-way up the mountain. Johnathan signaled to scout the surrounding area.

"Don't go too far off," Johnathan warned, disappearing into the thick brush.

Mel nodded to herself and walked out into the woods. Pushing back branches and inspecting the ground for any sign of disturbances. Lifting up a rock a beetle scurried away causing her to drop the rock and whip her hands on herself in disgust.

The sun sent beams of light through the tree line like golden ribbons. It had to be afternoon as they continued the search with no traces of human life.

Mel sat under a tree and scanned the sloping terrain slowly. A large yellow and black butterfly caught her eye and when it landed on a branch close by she went to get a better look at the insect. But the butterfly took flight again; she turned to go after it when something small and white caught her eye, flapping in the hot breeze.

The wind picked up again and she clamped her hand over her nose at the sudden, disgusting smell. Something in the area was sickeningly sweet. Taking a tentative step forward, she emerged in the clearing. The smell was stronger here, lingering, thick like a musk or miasma, making her close her eyes to stop them from watering. A tentative look at the space had her calling for Johnathan.

Chapter 18

What stood in front of Mel wasn't a naturally made clearing. The area was destroyed, appearing like a severe storm had blazed through. Trees lay uprooted and smashed to pieces. The hard earth was torn open and dark splotchy stains littered the area covering the ground and trees. She walked to the tree, snapped in two where the rancid smell was the strongest, and picked up a piece of what appeared like more cloth. Screaming, she dropped it when her fingers touched the smooth, leathery, scaly, and dry material. Taking a few steps back, she tripped on a branch and fell onto her rear. She let out a small hiss of pain as her companions entered the area.

Johnathan had a hand on the hilt of his sword as he surveyed the area, alert for any sign of danger.

Tsume knelt beside Mel.

"What happened?" she asked as Johnathan took in the damage of the clearing.

He walked over and picked up a piece of that scaly material, hard lines set in his face. He tossed it to Tsume, and she made a similar grimace as recognition flashed in her eyes. The two proceeded to have a silent conversation with knowing looks.

"Mel, start heading down the mountain. You have enough daylight to make it back to the town," Johnathan said, brushing a hand over one of the smashed trees inspecting the damage.

"What! Why?"

"I'm with John on this. The mission just got more dangerous. If it was bandits, that would be okay, but..." Tsume trailed off, sending Johnathan another look.

"Why is the situation more dangerous suddenly?" she snapped, not liking these meaningful glances between her companions.

"For your first mission, I was hoping for something involving humans. But this is the work of a demon and a dangerous type to boot," he replied.

"Isn't that what my training has been for? I won't get in the way, I promise!" she begged, clapping her hands in front of her face.

Johnathan's eyes were soft as he placed a calloused hand on her head. A sad smile creased his lips as he spoke. "I know, but for this, it'll be much safer for all of us if you are off the mountain. Don't worry, the demon won't go after you, it just fe.."he stopped when he saw Tsume make an x sign with her forearms. He cleared his throat and started again. "The demon won't be interested in you. Just head straight to the town and wait for us to return. There's enough money for you to stay at one of the inns until then."

"Bu-"

"Melosia, don't argue, just go!"

Mel slinked back at his tone and gave Tsume a desperate glance, but Tsume turned her head to the side, shrugging.

Mel's face flushed and her lip trembled. Clenching her fist she muttered dropping her shoulders. "Fine."

Mel watched her dusty leather boots kick up dust and rocks. A well placed kick sent a gray pebble careening into the underbrush. A flash of brown rushed around, startled by the disturbance. A small smile twitched on her face despite her mood as she stalked over to see nothing but sloping terrain. Sighing for what felt like the hundredth time since she was sent down the mountain, she turned, almost stepping on a small black snake. Jumping back, her foot caught the edge of the slope. She threw her arms out forward in a desperate attempt to catch her balance, but the motion was too late. Her foot slipped, and she tumbled down.

She rolled and flipped until finally she came to a dense patch of vegetation where the ground leveled out. The wilderness seemed to bear down on her. Mel had no idea where she was, everything blended together. She tried to figure out which way would lead back to the mountain path, but nothing stood out. A hawk called, its clear voice cutting through the stillness of the trees, making it dawn on her how utterly alone she was. A shiver ran down her spine as she decided on a direction to take.

The sun was starting to set, amber light glistening through the trees. Mel felt a chill despite the muggy air. Her mind kept creating images of what could have shed that skin in the clearing. In the back of her mind, she knew what it was, but didn't want to admit it. A branch cracked in the distance making her flinch. She rushed to a ridge so she could look over, and get her bearings. Her stomach dropped as she gazed out.

Logically speaking, getting off a mountain should be easy: Just head down and you arrive at the base. Yet, as she stared out, Mel realized she was higher up the mountain than when she started. In the dimming sun-light, the town appeared as just a small speck in the distance.

Mel was so lost. There was no way she would make it off the mountain before the night fell.

Setting her jaw, she searched for a nice secure area to set up camp. At least she had her rucksack. She pulled out her brown plush sleeping bag. Then she collected some large stones to make a lopsided circle for a fire pit. She placed small twigs in the center and left the camp to search for larger fire wood.

She returned with an armful of reasonably sized sticks, the bark scratching her arms as she walked. A rustling in the bushes made her turn her head and there was that flash of brown again. Her hair stood up. Was something following her? Could it be the demon? Her body gave an involuntary shudder and she dropped the sticks. Shaking her head to clear out those thoughts, she squatted down to recollect her firewood. With the scale of the destruction, the demon was large, so it was probably just a rabbit, she thought, continuing to her camp.

A soft gurgling hiss drifted to her ears. Now she was shaking. Taking a deep breath to calm her rattled nerves, she placed the wood down and stalked toward the sound to learn what she was up against. Gingerly pushing the branches of a tree aside, she discovered a crystal clear river being filled by a small waterfall rushing down the side of a cliff. A sigh of relief escaped her lips as she placed a hand on her chest. She drank from the water and gazed at her disheveled face. She splashed the crisp cool water on her face, then combed her sticky bangs down.

"Time to get back to camp, almost dark," she said to herself, wanting to break the silence that settled around her.

Mel's mouth dropped when she returned to her camp. Her bag laid to the side, the contents spilled across the ground as a family of fat raccoons sat eating her dinner. They paused, staring at her with their beady eyes. In a flash, they scattered, grabbing everything with their greedy little paws. They scampered up the trees with Mel close behind, snarling like a beast.

"Get back here you evil little fiends!"

Sadly the raccoons were faster and more agile in the tree branches and in a matter of seconds, Mel lost them. She sat for a few seconds punching the trunk of the oak she sat perched on. Grumbling, she accepted her loss and scrambled down the tree. She kicked her now empty bag in frustration, plopping onto her sleeping bag.

"At least they didn't steal my bed," she said bitterly as she piled up her firewood again.

"Now for fire." She concentrated on the pit, taking deep calming breaths. She pictured fire and pointed at the sticks, waving her hands. Maybe it was her irritation at everything that had transpired in a single day, but the fire exploded to life in a brilliant blaze. Shielding her eyes, she jumped back as the fire died down to a small flame.

Collecting what was left from the raccoon raid, Mel took inventory. A small water flask and a singular small piece of jerky.

She snarled, ripping a chunk off with her teeth and chewed, slowly watching the flames. When she lay down in the stuffy sleeping bag, she was plagued by thoughts like whether raccoons were edible and if giant snakes existed, but finally she drifted off. Her dream was of beady-eyed raccoons, then it changed to that of a blurry image of a boy reaching out to her.

Something wet dripped onto Mel's face, stirring her from her dreams. She was greeted by the early misty dawn. The drips kept falling; she glanced up seeing that it was coming from the tree overhead. She couldn't make out what it was, she just hoped she wasn't getting peed on by raccoons. If so, she would settle her hungry stomach on raccoon stew. Bringing a hand over her eyes to get a better view, something wet and slimy fell onto her lap. She jumped up, slamming her head on the tree with a shriek. Clutching her stinging head, she stared in disbelief at the fish that flopped about on the ground in front of her.

Chapter 19

The fish flopped back and forth as Mel stared aghast. A million questions flew through her mind. Another silverfish hit her on the head as it fell from the heavens.

She yelled toward the sky, clutching her stinging head. "Que diablo!?"

A soft meow answered her back. Mel's eyes went wide as a kitten jumped from the branches, landed on her shoulder, and then onto the ground next to the fish. Its brown spotted fur was dirty, but its yellow eyes gleamed like golden honey in the morning light.

Mel was flabbergasted. It was the kitten that she helped not so long ago. *Did you follow me*, she wondered. A growl escaped from her stomach as she wrapped an arm around her middle. The kitten proceeded to pick up one of the fish and drop it at her feet, meowing. Then it ran to the other fish, made a motion at Mel, and then ripped a chunk out of it, staring at the girl expectantly.

"Is....is this for me?" She felt stupid talking to the kitten as if it would understand. To her surprise, the kitten nodded its little head, its pointed ears flopping with the motion. Mel stared, mouth agape. She blinked, lifting up the squirming fish.

"Thank...you."

Grabbing a sharp stick, she stripped the bark off with her saber and skewered the fish, letting it roast over the smoldering embers of her dying fire. She felt something warm by her leg and glanced down to see the kitten dragging over the fish that it had not eaten yet. It looked up at her expectantly as if waiting for Mel to eat as well.

Once the stick was burnt black and the fish's skin crisped and curled, Mel pulled it off. After waving the fish to cool it down, she took a bite of the flakey flesh She proceeded to savagely rip into it. The sound of crunching at her side signaled the kitten had begun to eat.

With food in her belly, Mel yet again tried making her way down the mountain this time following a worn game trail. As she walked her steps were accompanied by the rustling of small paws through dirt and old leaves. She stopped as did the kitten who looked up at her. She took a few tentative steps as the kitten followed suit. It was following her.

"You're pretty smart," she said, bending to scratch it behind the ear. "If you're going to continue following me, I guess I should name you. Maybe I can convince Johnathan to let me keep you. I know Uncle wouldn't mind."

The kitten meowed as if it were ecstatic, and bounced up and down in a circle. Mel sat down under a tree, cupping her chin in her hand.

"I don't know if you're a boy or a girl." She paused as the kitten nodded.

"Boy?" she asked. The kitten sat still. "Girl?" The kitten nodded.

"I think I've finally lost it. What about a name? Spot, Kitty, Fluffy..." Mel went on listing the most basic of names for a cat as the kitten shook her small head.

"You're being too picky, you know. Okay, what about Flora? No. Mittens? Not that one either! You look like a little savannah cat. Would that work?" The kitten ran in a circle.

"What, Savannah? You like that name?" she asked as the kitten ran to her side, purring.

"Savannah it is. Come on, let's find the actual path and get out of here."

The sunlight now streamed strongly through the trees, sending beams of cascading light through the foliage. Going by her inner clock, Mel would have guessed it was noon. She pushed some more thick branches out of her way and stumbled into another clearing. Dusting herself off, she looked around and let out a sigh of relief. Finally, she had made it back to where she had started. Sitting on one of the broken trees, she took a swig from her canteen and then poured some out for Savannah.

"Okay, Savannah, let's get off this mountain," she said, running toward the earth packed trail.

She had made it a little down the path when something startled Savannah. The kitten jumped, running in-between and under Mel's feet. Mel did her best not to step on or kick the kitten, but stumbled backward. She landed too close to one of the many sloped ledges, and the eroded earth caved under her and she fell down the mountain for a second time.

Frantically, she grabbed at anything to stop her slide. But everything slipped or ripped itself from her hands. Down and down she went. Dirt and grass got into her eyes and mouth as she clawed for purchase. Finally, she slammed onto some packed flat ground. She groaned. A small mass landed hard on her stomach, making her explode in a fit of coughs. She shot a dirty look at the kitten who turned her head to the side in a cute manner.

Mel stood and dusted herself off. Taking a look at the clearing she had landed in, she spotted a dark cave, its opening like a gaping mouth. She took a step back at the smell when it hit. It was putrid; the smell of rot, and it clung to the air like death. She took another step , having felt a chill run all the way through her body. Savannah let out a small hiss, her fur on end making her appear like a small cotton ball. Taking another slow step back, Mel stepped on something and a loud crack seemed to echo through the clearing.

Mel's stomach twisted as the smell intensified. The smell of death was coming closer. It was almost like tangible claws reaching out extending for her. A sound came from the cave and grew louder.

A slinky man stepped out of the cave into the light. His green, slicked-back hair shone with a greasy gleam like it hadn't been washed for weeks. Mel held her breath. She should feel relieved, but something wasn't right. Savannah still appeared on edge, her fur sticking up and her tail lashing back and forth.

The man gazed at her with piercing yellow eyes. Casting her head down to appear smaller, she noticed what she had broken. It was a bone, a stained long, most likely not animal, bone. She swallowed thickly, feeling the man's lingering gaze.

The man seemed to sense her unease, and put on a pleasant smile that stretched unnaturally on his face. "Hello."

"He...hey, sorry for di...distubing, I mean disturbing you. I'm just a little lost," she said, irritated by her stuttering and shaking.

"How unfortunate, I can help you if you like." He took a step further into the clearing.

Savannah hissed, echoing throughout the clearing. She had squatted as if ready to pounce, her sharp claws extended out in warning. A loud growl rumbled in her throat.

"Ssorry about that. Catss have never seemed to like me," he purred out, slurring the s together.

"No, I...I should apologize. I'll go now," she said, finally stopping the shakes.

Mel's eyes darted around the clearing. At the entrance of the dark cave, she spotted something white, more cracked bones scattered about. Some of the bones looked like they had flesh still clinging to them. Flies buzzed around in small black clouds. Sweat started to form on Mel's brow as the breeze blew by, intensifying the putrid stench of rot that clung to the man. Every fiber in her very being screamed for her to run.

"No, no. Don't be like that. Stay, relax. We can have a small meal before you go." He continued his slow advance, making every step deliberately small, the creepy smile still plastered on his face.

"I really must leave, good day," she squeaked out, taking a step back.

"NO!" he snapped. Rage flashed across his face but was gone as fast as it had appeared. "Pleasse sstay for dinner."

At those words his smile stretched even further across his face as he began to change, getting larger and longer with every second. Dark green and brown scales gleamed in the sun like jewels as the man transformed into a giant snake. His head was almost as large as a small car, his body bigger than a house. He coiled his thick body around himself to rise up, towering over the girl making her feel like a mouse.

All the blood drained from Mel's face. She went as white as some of the bones that littered the area. Her eyes widened. Her stomach twisted. Terror ripped into her with iron claws. She began to tremble and shake uncontrollably. This couldn't be real. Why was it so big? Even the bear that attacked her wasn't this big!

"Now, now, child, I wonder what you taste like. I never give up the chance for a free meal," he hissed, giant yellow slitted eyes gleaming as his forked tongue lashed out tasting the air.

"Ay dio...Ay dio...Ay dios mio!" her voice croaked out and tears started to pour from her eyes. Her convulsions caused her knees to give out and she crumpled onto the ground, frozen in terror.

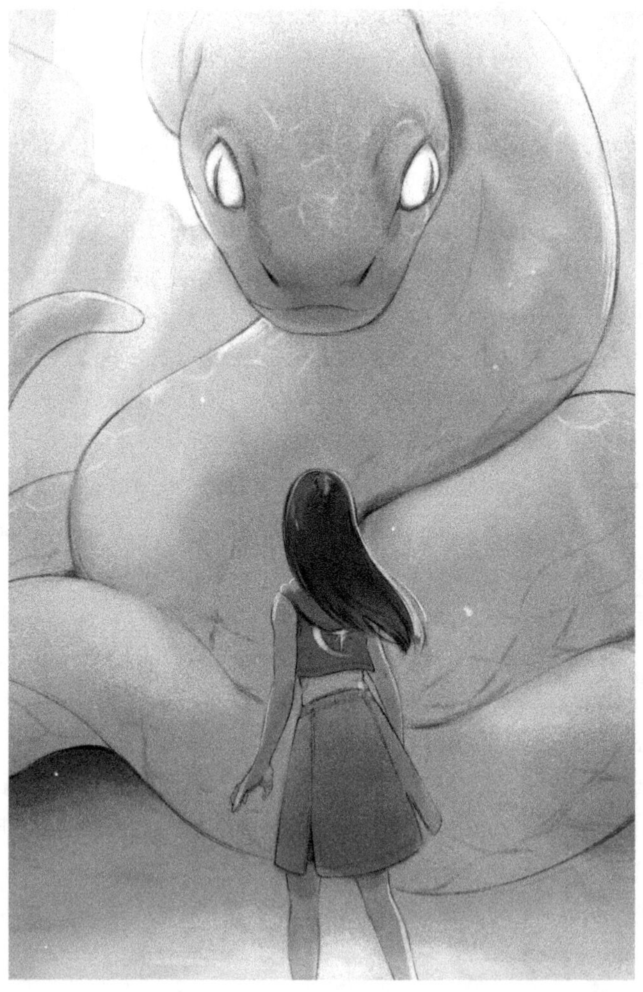

Chapter 20

Terror gripped Mel as she crawled backwards, rocks digging into her palms and hot tears spilling down her face as she shook her head. *No, no, no, no, no. This can't be real. I'm going to die. I'm going to die. I'll never see mom, Alma, or Daniel again. No,* she chanted the words over and over in her head like a screaming chorus.

"No. I do..do..don't want to die," she croaked out, her throat so tight she could barely breathe.

The giant snake seemed to relish her terror. He sat coiled up, watching her break-down with a glint of amusement as he hummed. He opened his mouth to reveal rows of long serrated teeth, longer than daggers.

Savannah roared, leaping in front of Mel. She opened her mouth releasing another fierce snarl. Despite the kitten's size, her roar echoed through the area. The unexpected noise caused the serpent to stop, it blinked curiously at the cat. In the blink of an eye, the kitten bit down hard on Mel's ankle, tearing through her boot and drawing blood. The stinging pain brought her out of her stupor; she bolted, throwing herself into the wilderness, running at a breakneck pace, with the kitten by her side. A sound like thunder resounded in her ears from behind. The ground shook and trees broke to pieces. Mel ran, choosing the dense foliage, hoping it would slow the monster down.

"You can't hide from me, little girl!" the beast roared in the distance.

Mel didn't turn back, she didn't slow down, she just kept running. Her breaths came out in hot stinging pants as she pushed herself onward. Finally, after building up the nerve, she glanced over her shoulder seeing nothing. Then her feet were on nothing. For a few seconds time froze as she looked to see that she had run straight off a ledge on a steep incline. She didn't have time to scream as she plummeted down the side of the mountain.

Pain erupted through her battered body as she slammed against rocks and trees. She clawed desperately at anything to stop her fall, but she kept rolling, tumbling, and spiraling, getting faster and faster. She was in the air again. Then, as she bounced off another ledge, she reached out her finger-tips, just grazing the edge. Then she plummeted again, straight into a thick bramble of bushes that broke her fall engulfing her. What little air she had was ripped from her lungs. She had landed on her back, and the pain was immense. Her breath came in shallow pants, her lungs searing with each gasp.

She wiggled her toes and fingers, and tried to rise, but she couldn't get her left arm up. It seemed to be stuck in the branches. She looked down and bile rose in her throat. Her hand was skewered with a broken branch right through the middle. Blood flowed slowly from the ghastly wood. Tears cascaded from her eyes as she gritted her teeth, grabbing her wrist to rip her hand off the branch.

Mel took a deep breath and closed her eyes. *I'm Melosia, student to Johnathan, slayer of deer, maker of fire,* she thought over and over psyching herself up. She wrenched her hand free. Blood poured onto the ground from the gaping hole. She made sobbing, croaking noises, and bit on her right fist to stifle the noise. She fought to stay conscious, ripping a piece of fabric from her skirt and wrapped it around her bleeding hand, like Johnathan had taught her. She wished he or Tsume were here. They would help her. Tears rained onto her hands, mixing with the smeared blood. She wanted to scream from the pain but she did all she could to stay silent, hidden in the thicket of bushes, curled up and trembling. If she made a noise, the snake would find her and she'd be eaten, but it hurt so very much.

Chapter 21

Mel lay in the thicket watching and listening through the dark green leaves. She didn't see any sign of the snake or hear anything; all was still. After taking a breath to prepare herself, she grabbed a branch to hoist herself. Her body was stiff from hiding.

Don't! Stay put or die, a voice said right in her ear. She turned to the side, frantically looking, but no one was there. Not even Savannah, her stomach twisted at the thought that the kitten might have gotten hurt. Mel shook her head, chalking the voice up to blood loss and terror, and went to leave the thicket again.

I told you to stay the hell still. He's close, the voice warned, so clear and close.

No one was there, yet she was sure that someone was talking to her. "Hello? Where are you?" she whispered, eyes darting around for any kind of movement.

Shut up, will you, the voice chided with a bored kind of urgency.

She instantly shut her mouth and a few moments later, the sound of crushed leaves cut through the silence. The snake man stalked out of the trees, walking only feet from her, scanning the brush, humming.

"Come out, come out, wherever you are." His yellow eyes darted back and forth, searching for any kind of movement.

Mel held her breath. The minutes ticked by as the man stood motionlessly, just watching, waiting. Then he spun on his heel and continued his search in another direction.

"Thank you," Mel whispered after a few moments, still uncertain on who had helped her.

No problem. Get ready to move, the voice replied.

"Wait, who are you and why are you helping me?" she questioned, making sure to keep her voice as low as possible.

Nobody that matters. Just a stranger passing through, and I thought it would be fun to try and keep your pathetic butt alive, like a game. If you want to live, stay quiet, think your thoughts, and do as I say. Now run and don't stop! The voice barked out.

Mel nodded and bolted. She didn't know why she was trusting this voice, but something felt right about it, like she could trust it. What other choice did she have?

Keep going. Don't stop moving.

She kept running, stumbling down the mountain. A sound of crashing echoed behind her and a chill went down her spine. The snake was on her heels, she knew it. She started to glance over her shoulder, her hair whipping around her.

Don't turn around! Stop and hide, the voice urged.

Mel didn't question the directions. She slammed her heels into the hard ground but she wasn't fast enough. In seconds the snake lunged forward, using his body to block her escape. Staring up at the snake's large mouth, Mel heard the voice cursing.

"There you are, my little treat," the snake purred.

You're going to have to fight, I'll try and help though it won't be much, the voice said.

Mel's fingers wrapped around the hilt of her saber. She pulled it out and pointed it at the serpent. She tried to put up a brave front, but it was ruined by the intense trembling of the blade flashing in the sunlight like a defective flashlight. Her hands were sweaty, making her have to adjust her grip, causing the shaking to worsen.

Very scary, the voice mocked.

Not helping, she thought back, leveling the saber's silver blade.

The snake lunged and she rolled out of the way. She got on her feet and slashed the snake. A small line appeared in the snake's green scales and a small stream of blood spurted out. A grin of pride grew on Mel's face, but it vanished as the wound steamed and sealed itself in a matter of seconds.

Don't stand still! Keep moving!

She rolled again as the snake snapped at her. Scrambling, she flipped out of the way of its tail. It was only by a hair's breadth, but she was keeping up in dodging the snake's attacks.

In a flash, the snake used his body to make a ring around her. She was stuck, trapped now as the snake loomed over-head. He opened his large mouth, fangs gleaming yellow-white against his red throat. He dove forward, prepared to eat her in one bite.

Thrust up! The voice commanded.

Mel moved like a puppet, driving her saber up. A disgusting squish and crunching sounded in her ears. The sword had gone through the head of the snake, stopping it from eating her. The wretched smell of rot and death surrounded her with every pungent breath that swished her hair steadily showing the snake was far from dead. Blood poured around her, hot and sticky. She held back a gag of revulsion.

The snake made a gurgling noise as he lifted his head, her sword still piercing him. Mel tried to hold onto her sword as her feet lifted off the ground. The snake thrashed his head back and forth.

The blood and sweat covering the sword's hilt made Mel's grip start to slip. She tried to regrip it, but the hole in her hand screamed back to life. Pain shot through her arm. Instinctively she released the sword and was flung into a tree and crumbled to the ground coughing. She rolled shakily onto her feet; she tasted iron on the back of her throat. She was unarmed, but that didn't mean she would give up. She lifted her hands. Using her fear and terror, she released a small fire ball and hurled it at the snake's snout colliding with a small pop. Smoke fumed and Mel heard a small sizzle but the snake just shook his head indifferently. She dropped her arms loosely to her side. They felt heavy, her whole body felt heavy and tired.

Was that the best you could do? The voice sneered.

Yes, that was my only trick, she thought back, her body going numb with dread.

It wasn't the time to feel self-pity or get involved in an argument with a voice in her head. She needed to stay focused, not get distracted. No sword or weapon and her magic had failed her. She had a bloody hand, probably some broken ribs. The odds were not stacked in her favor. Glancing around, she crouched ready to dodge and run when the time was right. Running away was the only thing she could think of doing.

Or you could just roll over and die.

Very helpful, she thought back bitterly, watching the snake's every movement.

The snake smiled, taking his time to size her up. "Iss that it for your futile resisstance?" he hissed. "How about I sshow you real power?"

Bringing his tail down, a vortex of air blasted past her, slicing her cheek. A loud crack followed as the wind ripped into a few trees, uprooting them and carving chunks out of the wood. Shredded leaves, needles, and bark rained down into the trench the snake's wind had created.

Clenching her fist, she thought, *is it petty that a snake monster is showing off his power before killing me?* It wasn't necessary at all.

A hiss roared as Savannah jumped from Mel's shoulder onto the snake's head and plunged her tiny claws into one of his yellow eyes. Blood spurted out like a fountain as the kitten rammed her claws over and over, slashing and clawing. The snake writhed in pain, dislodging the kitten.

Savannah landed gracefully in front of Mel, her paws and mouth covered in blood. She released a defiant roar. Mel sprinted, using the distraction to dive for the tree line, but in seconds she and the kitten were flipped and spiraling through the air from the snake's tail. She was caught in another cyclone of razor sharp air, tearing and slicing her skin like small blades.

"That'ss enough playing with my food!" the snake howled in rage.

Mel lay on the ground. Her last chance of survival had slipped away in an instance. Savannah lay to the side, trying to rise, her small body trembling with effort. *Any helpful advice?* She thought at the voice.

There was no reply. Mel gripped a handful of earth, gritting her teeth as she pushed herself into a kneeling position. Her vision was flickering and head was spinning. The voice in her head seemed to have even forsaken her. She braced her shaking body as the snake descended upon her. How could it have come to this again? Why was she so weak?

Chapter 22

M el looked death in the face, not wanting to back down in her final moments; to make Johnathan proud. The snake's bloody eye was healing but still oozed from the sides. As he slithered closer, time slowed down.

A sword whistled by her head, cutting a few strands of her hair and burying itself deep in the neck of the snake.

The snake reared back, screaming shrilly. The sound was terrible. The few birds that lingered took to the sky in a small black cloud. Savannah bounded back to Mel, hissing in fury. The snake spit foamy blood as he lunged again.

A white and blue blur jumped over Mel, spinning like a twister, and slammed a fist into the snake's snout, tossing it backward with an audible crunch. The snake crumpled as Tsume stood before Mel. She grinned at her, pulling off her outer blue shirt to reveal silver gauntlets with spikes glittering in the light.

Johnathan ran over and using Tsume as a platform lunged at the snake. He grabbed the sword sticking out of the snake's throat and ripped it out, leaving a gaping wound as blood sprayed onto the ground. The scream of pain and rage was so intense Mel covered her ears.

Johnathan drew his other sword as Tsume stalked forward. The snake hissed, curling in on itself and turned back into the greasy man. He pulled out a silver whip from thin air and unrolled it with a crack. "You all ssmeell of dog. Wolf tribe, thatss the only one left, right?" He hissed smiling with bloody teeth

"Dang it, John, you had the perfect angle to slice the head off. You failed me. A giant noodle is what we fight and you fail me," Tsume teased, not taking her eyes off the demon.

"I'll get it next time," was his cold reply.

"There won't be a next time!" the demon snarled, lashing the whip.

Tsume grabbed Mel, sending them both rolling through the dirt as the tree behind them splintered into a thousand splinters that pelted them like rain. Johnathan lunged forward and the clang of metal on metal rang and screeched as the two dueled. Whip and swords moved as extensions of the users bodies and a blur of sparks danced around them.

Tsume watched, her shoulders tense, then she jumped in, landing a crushing blow on the demon's cheek. There was a sickening crack as his head turned in an impossible angle. Retreating, he twisted it back with a snap and spit a volley of shattered teeth. He grinned as new teeth grew into the old one's place.

In a flash, the fight began anew. Mel sat watching, barely keeping up with the action. Swords, whips, and gauntlets gleamed and clashed, sparks and blood flew through the air like fireflies on a summer night. The fight was impossible. How could they win against something that healed almost instantly? She watched as the demon's arm was wrenched out of place and then twisted right back grotesquely. Her eyes landed on her saber a few feet away. She reached for it, grabbing the blood-soaked leather. Her fingers dug into the hilt. She felt useless as she watched.

Ice spears crashed through the earth, tearing into trees and flesh. A misty fog crept along the ground as the ice retracted, shattered, and rained down upon the demon. A twister of air wrapped around him, repelling the ice needles, sending them into the trees.

Johnathan whistled and the ice flew to his side, coating his swords as he slashed, sending a wave of ice at the demon, cutting into his leg. The wound healed slower than his others as frost spread up his leg.

The demon's and Mel's eyes met; he lashed the whip at her. She moved on instinct, diving into a kneeling position and raising the saber in an attempt to deflect the attack. The whip collided with the saber, her arms jolted and tingled from the impact as the sword shattered, slashing her with tiny razors. But it worked as the whip smashed into the ground inches from her side. She rolled onto her feet and ran toward the underbrush to the demon's side. He jerked his arm back to pursue her, but was stopped when Savannah's razor-sharp teeth sank into his ankle, causing him to stumble as the frost that covered his leg cracked splintering his skin.

Horror flashed across the demon's eyes as Johnathan lunged forward, arms crossed propelled by Tsume. In one fluid motion Johnathan sliced the demon's head clear off. At the same time, Tsume dove to Mel's side, pushing her eyes away. Mel heard a wet thunk as the head bounced on the ground and rolled into the shade of a half-smashed tree. The body collapsed and blood poured out.

Savannah crawled on top of the dead body and roared in triumphant victory. Mel peeked behind Tsume's arms, and watched the blood pool as the putrid smell of death, gore, and sweat over-took her. She ran to the side of the clearing, and vomited her guts out. Her body heaved and shook all over. A soft touch rubbed her back and pulled her hair back.

"There, there," Tsume hummed, "you did good."

"You did well to survive," Johnathan agreed, wiping the red off his swords and sheathing them. "Even though you were not supposed to be here," he added coldly.

Mel flushed at the accusation in his voice. Shaking, she took a breath. "I got lost. I didn't want to stay up here. I didn't go looking for the snake."

Johnathan looked her over, gauging the truth of her words. He took a few steps toward her and placed a hand on her head, ruffling her messy hair. Then he walked back to the body without another word.

Savannah released a growl. Mel called out to her. "Get away from that thing."

The kitten put her head down and scurried over to the girl's side. She rubbed her head against Mel's leg, purring.

"Did you keep our girl alive?' Tsume cooed, leaning over to scratch the kitten under the chin. "And we should thank you for that assist. Especially you, John."

"When did you come in contact with this demon?" Jonathan asked incredulously, ignoring Tsume's comments.

"She's such a cute little one too." Tsume continued to coo.

"Savannah's a demon? That explains a lot actually, I'm such an idiot. Can I keep her? She literally slashed the snake's face to ribbons to save me." Mel picked the kitten up to cradle her in her arms, a new wave of energy washing over her at the fact that she and the kitten were still alive.

"Come on, John, they obviously bonded. Savannah seems to be quite young, the perfect age to raise," Tsume replied, straightening up with her hands on her hips.

"They've bonded. There's nothing I can do about it," he said, looking the two over. "Mel, you can keep her. Tsume, take them both back to the village to get their injuries treated. I'll burn the body and head back later."

"I'm fine, I want to watch," Mel protested, swaying at the world that was rotating too fast underneath her, causing the other two to roll their eyes.

When Mel found herself being lifted up in Tsume's arms, she released a startled yip.

The trip down the mountain was quiet, Tsume didn't seem to have any problems carrying her. As the hike continued the adrenaline left Mel's body, making it grow heavy and weak. Her eyes began to close as she fought to stay awake. She drifted into a dreamless sleep.

Chapter 23

Mel opened her eyes. Her vision fizzled in and out, then settled to a white room with a small kitten sleeping on her stomach. Mel turned her head to the side to see Daniel slumped over, asleep in the chair beside her bed. Lifting up her hand, she saw it wrapped tightly in fresh white bandages. Laying her hand back down, she groaned. Her body was stiff and sore all over, but her back was the worst. *Falling off a mountain does that*, she thought, jokingly.

Daniel shifted, falling forward and waking with a start. When his eyes met hers, he beamed. "You're awake. That's good. I'm going to get old man Lupus and the others. I'll be right back," he said, standing up and then grabbing her hands. Then released them, apologizing when she hissed in pain.

As he left, Mel forced herself into a sitting position, gritting her teeth. Looking at the white walls of the room, it dawned on her that she was in the infirmary now. She patted Savannah gently and the kitten opened one golden eye and closed it, purring.

Lupus, Johnathan, Tsume, and Storm walked to her bed led by Daniel. Storm swooped over and started inspecting the bandages, checking her temperature, and making her move her creaking joints. A frown creased her brow as she moved items on the small side table, searching as she hummed.

"Good morning," Lupus said, smiling. "I heard you had a hard time on your first outing."

"If you call almost dying and falling off a mountain a hard time then, yeah," she rasped out, her voice painfully dry. Storm handed her a cup of water. The cold liquid was a blessing on her parched throat.

"I also heard that your survival was thanks to your new friend, Savannah?"

Mel nodded, not wanting to talk after hearing the awful state of her voice. Savannah sat up meowing as something glittered underneath her belly.

"That is not yours, little one," Storm tsked, snatching a vial from under the kitten and walking away.

"Johnathan has some questions to ask about what happened and I wanted to check up on you and our new pet," Lupus said, petting the kitten. "After that you can go back to sleep and recover your strength. That hand injury is quite nasty. You must have a great story to tell."

Mel nodded as he patted her head tenderly. He took his leave.

She began to explain how she had gotten lost and stayed the night on the mountain. She talked about running into Savannah and falling into the snake's lair. She even talked about getting robbed by raccoons, but she didn't utter a word about the voice. Something about that felt far too personal to share. After Johnathan finished his questions, Storm shooed him, Tsume, and Daniel away so Mel could rest.

The next few days were a mix of sleep, pain, and visits with a sprinkling of terrifying nightmares. Daniel and Lupus were her frequent companions, always stopping by during meal times to help if needed. Her face flushed at getting fed but it allowed her to rest her hands. Tsume and Johnathan appeared less often, but showed up all the same. Reginald even visited once to hear the story. He laughed hysterically about the raccoons and was chased away by Savannah; though it seemed more like play than a threat. Finally, the bandages were removed, leaving a small scar and her training was continued with the addition of Savannah by her side.

"Does having a single drop of demon blood or I guess genes really make you heal faster? It's amazing. Is that why my scar is disappearing already? I kind of wanted to keep it as a symbol of power," Mel said, panting on the ground with the kitten sprawled out next to her. "You know, a cool battle scar."

"Yes, you saw with your own eyes the regenerative powers a demon possessed. Even if the blood is diluted along our blood line it still exists to make us stronger. That's why the only sure way to kill a demon is to cut off the head or hope you wear down the regeneration completely," Johnathan explained, leaning over her. "Now stop trying to get out of coordination practice. Savannah is a baby and needs just as much instruction as you."

"Are you calling me a baby?" she whined indignantly, standing and snapping a finger in his direction. "Savannah, sic him!"

Mel and Savannah lunged, trying to take him on as a pair. The fight lasted about a second. Two swift blows took them both down yet again.

"You're not even trying at this point. Coordinating an attack with a partner is a good strategy in battle. Yelling sic him and bite his ankles is not," he chided, stepping back to avoid Mel's pathetic attempt to swipe at his ankles.

Sitting down in front of her, he made her look him in the eyes. "Look, I know you still feel the pain and fear of what happened, but take it as a learning experience of what is to come in the future. You won't be alone like that ever again. You have Savannah with you now. You are partners. Come up with attack patterns. We're done for the day."

Mel had thought about the snake attack for days now and how she was utterly defeated and at his mercy. When all her tricks failed her, she needed to have an ace up her sleeve. Thankfully, it was Savannah, but what about the next time? She had a fair idea to work on, but couldn't do it alone.

Mel's skin tingled with nerves as she pushed open the tavern door, spotting the person she was looking for standing in the back.

"Evening, Reginald. What fine weather-"

"Stop right there. What do you want? You never talk like that," he questioned, crossing his arms, tapping a finger impatiently.

"I was thinking I need to have a backup battle plan in the future, so I was wondering if," she paused, blurting the words out. "You could teach me to throw knives."

Reginald stared, dumbfounded. She could see the cogs ticking and spinning in his head. He cocked his head to the side, faking indifference. "I don't know, I'm pretty busy."

"Doing what, throwing darts at a board in a pub by yourself?"

"You shouldn't sass someone you want something from. Maybe if you beg and apologize I'll consider it."

"Sorry, I just mean you are an amazing knife thrower, much better than anyone else I know. You're the only one I can rely on for this," she said, holding her hands together pleadingly, trying to butter him up.

"That is true." A small smirk appeared on his face as he pushed his auburn hair back. Mel grinned, knowing she had him. "But I don't know if I can; there'd be nothing in it for me."

Her shoulders dropped. She rubbed her temples, knowing what she had to do. Turning to the side, she didn't look at him as she said the next words, not wanting to see his smug face. "If you help me I'll ask Johnathan to let you join our training sessions some times."

"Well, if you put it that way. From what I've heard, you did show quite a pathetic display in the mountains and could use some of my expertise."

The rivals shook hands in agreement. Reginald started right away, instructing her how to throw darts correctly. They spent the rest of the evening practicing while Savannah drank milk from a small bowl, watching with eager golden eyes, scoping up a discarded dart placing it next to her bowl.

Chapter 24

"That was intense. A good thing that lovely face wasn't damaged," Dj sang, as the group sat along the table at the tavern.

"You should be glad that she's alive. You freak," Spike snapped, reaching across the table to smack Dj.

"It's fine, Spike," Mel said, chuckling. "It was terrifying, but I learned where my abilities stand at the moment. And where I need more training." She filled a small bowl with warm frothy cream for Savannah.

"You even got a demon to boot. She increases your cute factor." Dj said.

"Must you always be like this?!" Spike rolled his eyes.

"Come on guys, don't argue," Daniel chipped in, trying to play peacemaker. "Actually, what do we have to thank for this visit?"

"Bandits," Spike answered nonchalantly, pointing with his fork.

"Bandits?" Johnathan asked.

"Bandits."

"Spike," Dj said, "not everyone speaks in only one word or insults. Stop being cryptic. There have been rumors of bandit activity to the east of you. It's out of your territory so you might not have heard, supposedly it's a huge group of thieves. I asked if Spike wanted help, and we decided to see if anyone here wanted to come along." Dj gave Mel a meaningful look.

"Johnathan?" Mel asked.

"No. You just went on a mission."

Silence fell over the table. Everyone stared at Johnathan. He stared back indifferently to their pleading glances. He didn't even flinch at Spike's arctic gaze. He looked Mel in the eye, studying her. He picked up his glass and stirred the liquid inside. Sighing, he fixed a flat look at the members at the table.

"You swear you'll watch out for her." It wasn't a question, more like a demand with a threat underneath. "And Daniel will go as well. He's got a gift for breaking up your fights."

"That was surprisingly easy. What's the catch?" Mel asked, squinting at him with suspicion.

"No catch. After a little thought, it seems a good and relatively simple experience with no demons at least the kind I wanted your first outing to be like. Sadly, I won't be able to come along because of Lord Lupus this time. This is one of the reasons why Daniel is going. And also, Dj if you do anything to my student, I'll end you painfully," Johnathan said, and the last part had a suffocating cloud of malicious intent.

The soup in Dj's spoon spilled out as he stared wide-eyed at Johnathan. He was only able to nod in reply. Johnathan's evil smile turned charming in an instant. "I'm glad you understand. Give me the details later. Good day."

The next morning the group was off. They rode on horseback, the mountain chain at their backs. Towards the end of the day, they passed into a plain with a large lake. Its calm, dark blue surface glittered in the afternoon sun. They stopped to water the horses and then rested for a bit, sitting on the piles of large smooth rocks that littered the edge of the lake. The whole time they rested, Spike gazed intently into the distance across the flat surface of the lake.

"Let's rest at that tavern tonight," Dj said after they had begun riding again. He pointed at the wooden building with green and red banners waving in the wind.

"We can camp in the woods. Why waste money when we are hunting bandits in the woods anyways?" Spike jerked his head towards the dense foliage some easy behind the tavern.

"Come on. I'll handle the money; anyway how can you make a beautiful young lady like Melosia sleep on the ground?"

"I actually like the woods. The smell is comforting."

"Fine. What about Daniel? He is a delicate little flower."

"I am quite delicate."

Spike shot a dirty glance at Daniel and kept bickering with Dj. Eventually, Spike shrugged with a jerk, giving up and stomping toward the tavern leaving the horses to the others. He yanked the door open and all but threw himself into an empty chair towards the back of the crowded building.

After tending to the horses, they entered the large wooden tavern. It had an empty floor for dancing while the seats at the tables were full of dining travelers. A small group of bards sat in the corner playing their instruments for a couple that swayed on the floor.

Daniel nudged Mel, glancing at Dj who had pranced over to the bards and was striking up a conversation. "You're either going to love or hate this," he said, as a violin passed hands to Dj.

Dj strummed a few notes and a hush fell over the tavern like a magical veil had been raised. He pulled the violin up and began to sing. The notes of the strings resonated with his voice, which was like silk and warm honey, alluring and hypnotic. Everyone was enraptured by the sound. The other musicians started to play and sing. The patrons rose from their seats, mystified, and began to dance in circles, passing partners back and forth.

Mel felt a tug and found herself dancing as well. She was a puppet, not in control of her movements as the music guided her, her puppeteer. Daniel grabbed her hands as they spun, dancing faster and faster. Everyone was singing, dancing, and chanting. To the side, a dazed bar maid walked to Spike and dropped a key in his hand. He nodded at Dj before slipping up the stairs.

The dancing lasted for some time. Mel lost track of time. So many faces of dance partners passed by in a blur. She danced on the tables and in a circle, around and around. Her legs were tired and she was out of breath but the hypnotic melody kept control of her.

Dj finished his playing with a flourish. The room exploded with cheers as many cried for ale and beer. With a small nod he signaled for Mel and Daniel to follow him up the stairs to the room Spike had left for.

"What the heck was that?" Mel asked, collapsing into a heap onto one of the beds.

"Music magic. It's rare, and the levels of hypnotic control it has are ridiculous. As you felt," Daniel replied, falling on his stomach next to her.

"That's why his voice was so unnaturally beautiful," Mel said in wonder, staring at Daniel. He nodded with a slight grin.

"My voice was already amazing to begin with. The magic just added to it."

"Keep telling yourself that," Spike retorted, leaning against the doors. "Go to sleep. We're getting up early before the owner catches on to your little trick to get a free room."

"Wait a second, is this another sleep and dash?!" Mel cried, lunging from the bed.

Daniel rolled off the bed, laughing with Dj, as Spike rolled his eyes.

"I'm being serious. This is the second time in my life this is happening." She groaned, crawling into her bed and pulling the blanket over her head as Savannah curled around her neck.

"You should be used to it with your uncle," Spike said, walking to the corner of the room. "Get some rest," he added, blowing out the candles.

The next morning they took a hard left back toward the thick treeline of another forest that seemed to cover the land like a mat behind the tavern. After a long day of riding, they stopped and set up camp in a small clearing near a shallow creek as Mel and Dj groaned about their backsides hurting.

"This is the perfect spot. We'll appear like sitting ducks for the bandits and they'll strike," Spike said, reclining on a tree as he sharpened his curved daggers.

"Oh, fun. Camping with a side of murder is always a treat," Dj said, stirring a pot over the crackling fire Mel had made. The smell of smoke wafted through the crisp woody air, making it cloudy.

"You make it sound like a bad horror book. Isn't murder taking it a little far?" Mel replied, taking a seat next to Daniel on a fallen log with patches of green moss as they watched Savannah splashing through the water, chasing minnows.

"They're bandits, they know what they signed up for," Spike retorted, fixing a sharp gaze on her.

She looked away, not able to maintain eye contact. "They might be bandits but they must have their own reasons."

She shrunk in on herself when Spike rose sharply and walked past her. He shot her another look. "Believe what you want. Some things just have to be done."

Mel watched as his back disappeared into the shadows of the trees. After picking up a small twig, she started to draw in the dirt, pushing away leaves and grasses. Savannah came padding over with a small fish flopping in her jaws. She was drenched, holding her head up in triumph. The sun had started setting, darkening the shadows that lingered around them. The smell of smoke in the warm air and the sounds of creatures making their ways to their dens made Mel release a small sigh. A small twinge in her gut made her frown.

"What's on your mind; is it the snake demon still?" Daniel asked, scooting closer to her, hesitantly placing a hand on her knee.

Mel turned, giving him a small smile. "No, not that. Just thinking about my family. We would camp a lot when I was younger."

"You don't talk about them much. Do you miss them?"

"Of course but thinking about them is enough for me. I know they'll be fine. How about you? You've never mentioned your family?"

Daniel went silent. A strangled look crossed his face as he withdrew his hand and stared at his feet. "Don't know."

"I'm sorry, I shouldn't have pried," Mel apologized, taking his hands in hers to give him some form of comfort, not liking the sad look on his face.

"It's nothing to apologize for. I was abandoned at a young age and taken in by your tribe. Not that bad of a life," he replied, looking up at the sky as it darkened and the stars started to appear, squeezing her hand gently.

They sat in silence, watching the stars. Mel cast a worried look at Daniel, not knowing what to say to him. Should she let go of his hand? Had she overstepped boundaries? Yet he seemed content, staring at the stars, his hand warm in hers. A small rustle of bushes announced Spike's return, breaking the small spell as they unclasped hands.

"Didn't see anything suspicious or smoke from fires," Spike said, taking a seat next to her and casting a doubtful look at Dj as he handed out bowls of rice.

"We are in the right place. The forest trail here has been a hotbed for this group of bandits," he replied, defensively taking a seat next to Daniel. "You should be happy that I'm helping. This wood isn't near my tribe's domain."

"I don't need your help. It was a request from an ally," Spike snapped back.

"Don't argue when there are people in the crossfire," Daniel whined, clapping his hands together. "I know let's have a game for Mel to figure out what tribe everyone is in."

"That sounds like fun, I want to go first."

"Like I care. Does Mel even know what tribe she's in? Knowing Lupus he probably didn't tell her."

"Uncle didn't tell me. But I'll take an educated guess on the wolf because an unnamed source that tried to eat me said it as a kind of insult," she replied, scratching the back of her head.

"Ding! Ding! Ding! That's correct! Now guess mine. I'm a beast of legend and song. I'm magical and can fly. What am I?" Dj said, striking a pose.

Mel brought her hand to her mouth in thought. His description was kind of random, so she guessed the first thing that popped into her head. "A unicorn."

"That's right I am a majestic unicorn...No! I'm a dragon, a dragon!" he yelled, flapping his arms like a deranged pigeon. "My mom's a dragon! That's pretty cool, right?! Stop laughing!"

"How does that even work?" Mel muttered, glancing at Daniel who had fallen off the log, laughing and clenching his sides.

Spike was doubled over, too. "That was hilarious! You said that with such enthusiasm, you overgrown lizard."

"Yeah? Let's see her guess your tribe next, fuzzy."

"Fine. My tribe is known as one of the fastest," he said, calming his laughter, then pointing at Savannah who was chasing after the flying sparks of the fire. "Feline."

"Not fair! That's way too obvious!"

"Like I care."

"A cheetah?" Mel replied, uncertain if it was a trick.

Spike nodded, crossing his arms. "Right. Daniel's next."

"It's not really a tribe if you're the only member," he replied, with a sad smile, taking his seat again.

"Go ahead," Dj said, patting his back.

Daniel sighed. "Okay so canine tribe, not brave or sly; just cowards," he said, self-deprecating.

"Coyote," Mel said almost instantly. For some reason, it felt like it fit him. Maybe it was the hair.

His reply was a sad smile.

"I actually have always thought coyotes were pretty cute," she added, quickly, causing him to flush and look away.

Dj kept them entertained by singing different lullabies for a while. Then they pulled lots for the night watch. Mel was exempted much to her disapproval. In the end the first watch was shared between Mel and Daniel, Spike had the second, and Dj had the last.

As the other two slept, Mel and Daniel sat close to the fire, watching the sparks lift into the dark sky like dancing fireflies. It was silent except for the insects of the night and the occasional hooting of an owl or Dj's soft snores. They didn't speak, just enjoyed one another's company as they watched for danger while the night drifted by.

Chapter 25

A soft thud echoed throughout the camp as Mel's knife embedded itself into the trunk of an oak tree yet again. She threw another that hit only a few inches from her other knives that made a lopsided circle, or maybe a square, it was hard to tell. A sigh left her lips; she was still not very good at it even if she now had the basics down. She walked to the tree and yanked out the knives one by one to try and start again.

"Those were some okay throws," Spike said, leaning on another tree; his voice emphasized the okay, making her wrinkle her nose.

"Thanks?" she replied, walking back to her place in front of the tree. Relaxing her shoulders, she threw the knife. It hit close to the branch she had aimed for.

"Here's some advice. You need to relax more, feel the knife as an extension of your body and not just a tool. Let the movement flow," he said, walking over. In one fluid motion he threw one of the knives impaling a leaf to the trunk.

Mel's eyes widened at how natural he made it appear and clapped her hands in praise. Spike smirked, pushing his fingers through his bright blond hair. "Come on, enough playtime; it's time to bait out those bandits."

The group walked along the winding forest trail, pulling the horses behind as they went. Their eyes scanned the trees and shadows for an ambush. A bird called, a skunk scuttled by, and to Mel's newfound distaste, a snake slithered into the underbrush, but those were the only signs of life the group had encountered so far. Tension was in the air. It was obvious that Spike's mood was going sour, judging from the way his dark eyebrows creased as he glared ahead.

They decided on a new plan, to split up. Spike and Dj would continue on the trail with the horses to act like the perfect bait; while Mel and Daniel would go off the trail and cover them, while searching for clues.

As they walked, Mel frequently looked over her shoulder, ready to run, fearing what the shadows could be hiding. Savannah must have felt her master's unease, because her ears stayed perked up, listening and alert.

When the shadows of the trees grew longer, Daniel and Mel set up camp.

That night, on her watch. Mel wondered if there even were any bandits. The forest seemed so peaceful. She jerked when Daniel's head fell onto her shoulder, then smiled at his sleeping face. She leaned back to get more comfortable on the tree, not having the heart to disturb him. Her eyelids grew heavy and she drifted off, with her cheek pressed against the top of his head.

A loud snap of a stick startled her awake. A figure stood before her, his silhouette framed by the light from the fire's dying embers.

Suddenly, there was a flash of silver as he drew his arm back, and Mel reached for her saber as a scream echoed through the air.

Savannah dug her fangs into the attacker's arm, and he stumbled falling to the ground. Mel lunged forward, drawing her sword, seeing two more men circling at the edge of the camp. Daniel pulled out a small dagger with a slight tremble, after being startled awake from falling over. Mel pointed at the dying fire and it exploded back to life, illuminating the scene.

The haggard men stood in the clearing. The one Savannah had mauled, arm now dripped blood from having succeeded in wrenching the cat off. The injured man and another lunged forward with swords as Mel intercepted. Metal clinked under the night sky as the three dueled. Mel parried one man's sword and drove her elbow into the other man's gut, sending him toppling to the ground. Spinning, she slammed the hilt of her sword into the first man's face, breaking his nose, with a disgusting crack. Turning she saw that the third man had overpowered Daniel and pressed a knife to his throat. Daniel stared at her with wide eyes.

"Drop the sword little girl. We'll be taking it along with your belongings. Also be a good girl and get on your knees," the man sneered, pressing the knife to cause a small cut.

Mel did as she was told and could hear a disturbance a bit off. Biting her lip knowing that must be Spike and Dj fighting. She was attempting to think of a plan when a sharp backhand knocked her completely into the dirt.

The man with the broken nose glared down at her with a twisted grin. "Let's have a little fun. I want to replay you for the nose," he said, digging his boot into her side.

Mel clenched her teeth as the man kept kicking her. She was grasping at straws in her head over what to do. She couldn't think of a plan when all she could do was curl up defensively. Cracking an eye open she saw a glint in the tree line as an arrow shot the man, holding Daniel hostage, in the arm. He howled in pain releasing Daniel.

Mel took the distraction. She swept the feet out from her assailant. Rolled to her feet and smashed her palm into the chin of the other. She stared down the third man, as he yanked the arrow from his arm, breaking it.

"Those cost a pretty coin, you know," the archer said, as he stepped out of the foreground another arrow notched and aimed at the bandit. Unlike the haggard bandits, he was clean cut with close cut dark hair that matched his skin tone. "You alright, kid," he added.

Mel nodded at a complete loss for words.

"I'm a bounty hunter. I'll take these guys in, as payment for the arrow and saving your lives," the stranger said, as Mel nodded again. "The others you were traveling with are up ahead you should go to them."

Mel grabbed her sword as she came to her senses. She could still hear fighting in the distance, and for a slight moment she debated whether to trust the stranger, but a glance at Daniel clutching his neck made her decide.

"Thank you," she said, heading toward the noise pulling Daniel behind.

"What about our things?!" Daniel protested.

"Dj and Spike could be in trouble, they're more important than some camping supplies," she paused pulling him to the side and did a quick once over of their surroundings. "Your neck let me see."

"It's fine, like you said they might need us."

"Daniel. You're just as important as Dj and Spike," she stated, gently removing his hand to examine the small cut. She ripped a piece of her clothes to wrap the injury.

"Not too tight, or you'll end up choking me," he teased.

She glared up at him, giving the cloth a small tug. "Don't make me get the chancla."

"Anything but the chanklatta."

She tsked. "You're doing it on purpose now."

He gave her a cheeky grin. "You need to give me a lesson, promise."

"Fine, I'll teach you a few words but you have to say them right," she sighed, taking his pinkie with hers.

Daniel grinned but it fell when he heard more shouting. "We should go. It's unlikely but they might need our help. And thanks Melosia."

Chapter 26

Mel bound through the foliage toward the clamor, clutching her saber with Daniel close behind. Crashing straight into the thick of it, Mel startled a bandit as she slammed her sword into his. As they dueled, Savannah lunged to her side, claws unleashed onto her master's enemies.

Dj and Spike stood back to back in the center surrounded by bandits. They didn't appear to need any back up as they effortlessly drove back any that came too close with knives and a large black and gold scythe, and despite their needless bickering the two made a good team, Dj's brute strength to back up Spike's agility and skill.

Mel took a quick glance behind to check on how Daniel was; he was struggling, being pushed back and stumbling. A knife flew straight into his attacker's forehead, making him crumple to the ground next to Daniel. Mel shot Spike a thankful glance as she continued to fight back the thieves on her end. She focused on disarming or breaking their old weapons. If a man tried to still fight her, she sent two quick jabs to their sides and a kick to the neck. Her breath came out in shaky puffs, but she held her own, and it gave her a small rush of mixed emotions. It wasn't an easy way to fight, but she didn't want the blood of others on her hands. So, was it wrong that she enjoyed the fighting and the challenge it provided?

The skirmish lasted for less than an hour. The air was thick with the stench of sweat and blood. By the end, some ran and Spike took chase, his daggers dripping crimson. Mel breathed heavily; sweat covered her in a disgusting film. She felt like a sewer rat. She gazed down at the man crumpled at her feet, clutching his forearm that dripped blood in a steady stream. She swallowed, her throat feeling scratchy.

"You've lost. There's no reason to die. Just come quietly. I don't want to kill you," she said with as much authority as she could muster.

The bandit dropped his head down, nodding, his hateful eyes covered by dark matted shaggy hair. Mel turned to go to the other two. With her back turned to him, the man lunged, ripping a knife out from the corpse of his fallen comrade.

Daniel's eyes widened as he surged forward. He tackled Mel as they slammed into the ground, the knife tearing into his shoulder. The man brought the knife up to stab them but screamed in agonizing pain as Savannah clamped onto the junction between his neck and shoulder. Blood spurted as the kitten ripped the flesh out, hissing furiously, driving her claws into his face. Mel watched in shock and horror, holding onto Daniel as the man rolled to his side, clutching his neck as blood poured out. Savannah leapt from his body, landing in front of Mel and roared.

The light faded from the man's eyes as he gurgled blood. Mel turned away, feeling sick by all the death. Her stomach plummeted further when she saw the blood pouring from Daniel's shoulder. She ripped more of her clothes and pressed it into the wound.

"I'm so sorry," she muttered, eyes casted down. "You saved me."

"It's fine, as long as you're not hurt and it can't be worse than the neck cut." He paused, looking at the gash and paled. "That's a lot of blood."

Daniel's eyes rolled back and he slumped into her arms. His body was warm and his heartbeat steadily in his chest. A relieved sigh escaped her lips as she hugged him. A short snort brought her attention to Dj.

"Typical Daniel. The sight of his own blood messes him up. Here." He squatted next to them. They leaned him against a tree as he snored lightly. Dj smiled at her, ruffling her hair.

Mel swatted his hand away and stared at the large scythe leaned against a tree. "Where did you even hide that?"

"This baby? In plain sight," he said, lifting up the scythe. He gave a quick twirl as the weapon shifted into a gold chain with a small music note charm. He put it around his neck and tucked it into his shirt with a wink. "See."

"How?!" she questioned, utterly baffled.

"Magic."

"Obviously!"

"Alright I'll explain, just don't make that face and put down the sword. The scythe was a present from my mom, she gave my sisters weapons too. It's a demons' weapon so it can change shape and mingle with the spirit realm and this one."

Mel stared at him making an 'Oh' face seemingly frozen in place.

Dj sighed, scratching the back of his head. "I'm guessing you have no idea what I'm talking about."

At the nod he received he started to explain in a know it all tone. "You see demon's can walk a thin line between the spirit realm and ours. It's how they are able to teleport and also why elementalists can transverse dimensions. It's how demons can summon their weapons out of thin air-"

Dj was cut off by Mel clapping her hands together. "The snake! He summoned a whip!"

"Yes, demons are apparently too lazy to carry their weapons so they use that little trick. The spirit realm is also where summoning demons stay until called upon, their own little pocket dimension they live in you can say."

"Do your sisters have scythes too? It's strange to think you have siblings." Mel crossed her arms looking up at him.

Dj gave her a smirk. "Naw, the scythe was either too scary or lame for them. I have three younger sisters. How do you think I became so charming?"

"I think you need to get your head checked. As an older sibling I can say it does not help charm," Mel frowned wondering what her sister was doing, was she getting good grades and watching out for mom. She missed them.

"Here comes Spike. Did you get them?"

"Yes," he replied. "Come up, let's get rid of the bodies. Do you think you can handle it?" he asked Mel, doubtfully.

She nodded, putting on a brave face.

The three pulled the bodies of the bandits into a pile. As Spike lit the fire to burn the pyre, Mel closed her eyes and bowed her head. She tried her best to ignore the acidic scent that burned her nostrils making her stomach turn with disgust.

"What are you doing?" the blonde asked.

"Praying for their souls. Before you say anything, I don't care if it's meaningless. I want to pray for their souls to find rest. They did bad things, but they might have had a reason and families," she said as she turned to Daniel who had just started to stir. "Let's go."

She helped Daniel onto his horse then felt something wet rub against her leg. Seeing the blood soaked kitten made her cringe away from Savannah in disgust. A look of hurt flashed in the kitten's eyes as Mel jumped onto her horse, keeping her back to her. "Stay away," she muttered.

"What's wrong with you?" Spike asked, as they rode in silence with Savannah sulking on his lap.

"Savannah ripped a man's throat out," Dj answered, as she kept her silence.

"Killings wrong," she whispered, stubbornly.

"That's it," Spike rode up close to her, staring her down. "Look, the cat's a demon. It's in her nature to kill. Death is a part of life here and you need to accept that. She was only protecting you."

As they rode on in silence back to Stella Luna, Mel kept glancing at Daniel and Savannah. Her heart felt heavy. She hurt them, both of them; she'd failed Johnathan, again. She was weak of heart, showing mercy and causing others trouble. Bitterness ran cold through her veins like ice water. Sagging her shoulders, she reached out an arm towards Spike. Savannah's ears perked up. She leapt to her master's side and rubbed against her check.

"I'm sorry," Mel apologized, scratching her. She swore to herself then not to let her family or friends get hurt again, she needed to steel her heart.

Chapter 27

Upon returning to the mansion, Mel locked herself in her room. She sat in the dimly lit room, huddled under her sheets, staring at the door. Every so often a soft knock would startle her but she refused to answer. She knew she was being selfish, locking herself away to sulk in the darkness of her room, but she couldn't help but dwell on her failure, the blood, and the death. The memory made her want to vomit. Everytime she closed her eyes she could visibly see the man's fearful eyes go dim as he desperately clutched at his throat as he drowned in his own blood.

She got away with this behavior for two days; eventually someone had started leaving a tray of food outside her door during meal times. Savannah had taken to hiding under the bed as she laid on her bed and wondered how long it would take until Johnathan got tired of this and forcefully dragged her out of her temporary sanctuary.

Her eyelids grew heavy, and then closed. Instantly the images of the man's fearful glare flashed through her head, startling her back awake.

"I didn't kill you," she muttered, pulling her knees to her chest. "And you tried to kill us. It wasn't my fault."

Savannah jumped onto the bed with a small bounce, snapping up what was left of her master's lunch. She meowed, looking at Mel with her gleaming, yellow eyes. An involuntary shudder ran down Mel's spine. She thought about how the kitten killed so easily. Shaking her head, she tried to rid herself of the thoughts, Savannah only did it to protect, and like Spike had said, it was only in her nature; she didn't know any better. Leaning her forehead against her knees, she tried to rid herself of the thoughts and doubts but she couldn't shake the fact the sweet kitten was a killer; a real demon. With that, the kitten scuttled back under the bed.

Mel scrunched up her nose. She was beginning to get irritated with the constant bed hiding. Flipping over the edge of the bed and yanking up the skirt, she was about to scold the kitten for her odd behavior but stopped at what greeted her.

Savannah sat upon a pile of various glittery objects, a hoard of mismatched junk; vials of empty medicines, jewelry, pens, quills, and silverware just to name a few. As Mel blinked, the cat pawed a dart underneath herself to hide it.

The ridiculousness of it caused Mel's grip to slip, making her topple out of bed. Snorting in laughter and pain, she rubbed her head. "This is why you've been sneaking around. You need to give this junk back."

Savannah stiffened, releasing a small mew with a trembling lip, causing Mel's heart to skip.

"Fine, I can't say no to that face. Take the jewelry back though, and this will be our secret," Mel said, climbing back into her blankets. "But no more stealing," she added, popping her head back under the covers.

Mel didn't know when or how, but she was walking through thick darkness. It was suffocating, squeezing around her from all sides, a deep and dark cavern of nothingness. She turned on her heels trying to find an exit. A blinding flash seared her eyes. Shielding her face, she blinked rapidly to readjust her eyes to the ever present darkness.

Two doors appeared before her. Taking a step back, she marveled at their beauty. Dark black wood accented with actual gold . The left door's gold was in the shape of snowflakes and the right like fire. She grasped the strangely warm handle of the right door and pulled it open.

A warm muggy breeze escaped, blowing her hair back. She took a step inside and felt hard stone under her feet. The only sounds that came from the darkness were her steps and the steady drip of something echoing off the walls. Drip. Drip. Drip.

Mel's hair prickled. She jumped back, hearing something shuffle in the darkness ahead. Large red eyes gleamed in the darkness. A cold fear overcame her. She fell to the floor, her fingers digging at the warm stone.

"What the hell do you think you're sulking about? Get over it! Your pet kept you alive; and some nobodies died. This behavior is boring. Stop sulking and move on!" a voice boomed, growling in the darkness.

Mel sat up in bed, breathing heavily, sweat dripping down her neck. Frantically she looked at her surroundings. Her room, she was in her room. It was just a dream, she thought wearily, rubbing her throbbing temples. Sighing, she got out of her bed. The blankets had been tossed to the floor. She made it to her door, planning on apologizing to Daniel for getting him hurt.

"I've wallowed in self-pity long enough." She pulled the door open and promptly crashed into another person, toppling to the floor.

"Crap, Mel are you alright?" Daniel asked, helping her up from the floor.

"I'm fine. I was actually going to look for you."

"I wanted to check up on you too," he said, releasing her hand all too soon. "What's up? How are you doing?"

"I'm sorry. I almost got us killed and you got hurt; because of my mistake." She looked at the floor, hanging her head while her shoulders sagged.

A weary smile graced his face as he affectionately ruffled her hair. "Don't apologize for showing mercy or kindness. That's what I..." he trailed off, pausing then cleared his throat, looking to the side. "Where's Savannah? I got her a gift."

Mel raised an eyebrow, deciding not to pry and to ignore the wishful feeling of what he was going to say, she whistled softly. The kitten sprung from under the bed, darting past the books and sheets that scattered the floor. She leaped onto the girl's shoulder and draped herself around her neck.

Daniel petted the kitten, then signaled to the small table in the room. The two sat down as Savannah rolled on the table showing her light tan belly. "You saved us back there thanks. I got you something," he said, pulling out a blue silk ribbon with a small silver bell attached. He tied it around the kitten's neck. When she shook her head, a soft note echoed through the air barely audible. She meowed, happily hounding around the table chasing the sound.

"It's lovely, thanks," Mel said, smiling. A warm feeling came over her as he smiled back, washing the chill that the nightmare had left away.

Daniel tapped a finger on the table. "You can teach me a few words. I can't wait to mess with Dj with not knowing what I'm saying."

"I did promise. Just so you know, I can understand it decently, but I never really got the hang of speaking it fluently like my mom, so I just speak broken spanish. Melosia's broken spanish lesson starts with Hola meaning hello, Gracias is thanks, Ven aqui means come here, Ay dios, Ay di, Ay di....," Mel's face turns a sickly pale at the feel of those words on her tongue, minding flashing to the taste of blood and a low hiss fills her ears, she froze vision tunneling and her breath caught.

"Mel, Mel, Melosia!" Daniel's voice cut through the fog reaching out to her. "What's wrong?"

"Sorry, I forgot the word. Continuing mi Amor means my love, Te amo means I love you, and lastly, Adios means goodbye," she spoke quickly, waving his concerned hand away.

The two sat speaking back and forth as Mel tried to help him pronounce the words correctly. It was childish but she felt a small twinge every time he said the phrases with amo correctly.

A rapid knock made them look to the door where Lupus and Johnathan stood. Mel felt her stomach twist at the thought of punishment for skipping training.

"I'm glad you're up and about now, I hope we aren't interrupting anything. I actually have some news for you," Lupus said, making a small gesture with his hands.

"And I am thoroughly against it." Johnathan glared at his leader's back, an icy bite in his tone.

"Come now, Johnathan, it's a good learning experience," he whined, wrapping an arm around his niece.

"Why has it been that every good learning experience has not ended well for her? Proving the point that I've been trying to make that she needs more training," he snapped back, crossing his arms as he stomped a foot to emphasize the last sentence.

"She would like to know what you're talking about," Mel said, raising her hand, causing Daniel to snicker into the back of his.

"I'd like to take you to the demon council with us next month," Lupus stated, nodding self-importantly.

"That'd be great!" Daniel beamed, grabbing her hands, but shrank back at the intensity of Johnathan's expression.

"I actually agree with Johnathan, on this," she said, casting her head down and slipping her hands out of Daniel's. "He's right. I got tossed off a mountain, almost eaten by a demon, a stake through the hand, and almost stabbed in the back. It seems trouble follows me everywhere I go."

"Look, Johnathan, you broke her spirit with your overbearing protectiveness. You're being a mother hen." Lupus pointed accusingly at him.

"I'm only looking out for my student's best interest," he said, turning away.

"Well, let's discuss this more in my office," Lupus said, dragging Johnathan behind him. He shot a wink over his shoulder that clearly meant he was up to no good.

"Poor John. He's going to be hounded until he gives in," Daniel said, picking up Savannah.

"I already said I don't want to go," she huffed, walking into the empty dark hallway. He hurried after her.

The dart hit the bullseye for the fifth time. Reginald smugly grinned to the other two's dismay. After leaving the mansion, Daniel had flagged down the red head and here they were now, losing horribly to the boy.

"I understand not wanting to go, after the last missions you've been one." Reginald sneered as he drank from his glass.

"You won't let it go will you?" Mel glared back.

"You got lost going down a mountain and ended up at the summit, that is something special." He grinned. "And let's not forget, falling off a mountain because you tripped on a cat," he added, then burst out laughing.

She gritted her teeth and waved her fist at him. "Let's go up the mountain so I can show you how funny it really is, Chupicabra."

"No, thanks princess. It's better if you don't go to the council anyway. Who knows what the saber-toothed tigers will do if you showed up." He had a dark smile as he leaned closer across the table. "People go missing all the time during the council because of them."

"Saber-toothed?" She raised an eyebrow while Savannah released a low growl.

"They do not. Violence is against the rules during the council," Daniel replied, uncertainty lacing his voice. "Stop trying to scare her. There's nothing to worry about. You're one of us and that's all that matters. I'd love it if you'd come along."

"What's that look for?" Reginald asked. "I was just messing with you. I think it'd be fun if you went along for the ride, much better than spending time with Tsume." He patted her head.

Mel scrunched up her nose, smacking his hand away. "I already said I don't want to go," she replied, glancing at the fire as more wood was added, sending up a cascade of sparks.

Reginald rose and pulled out the darts for the next game, a gleam in his eyes. "Fine, let's bet on it. If you win this round, we'll drop it. If Daniel wins, you agree to go, and if I win, hmmm, if I win, you're my servant."

"That's childish and unrelated to the situation," Mel jumped up to point at him.

"I just don't care either way. You game, servant?" he purred condescendingly, leaning over her.

She stood up straighter. "I liked princess better. You're on Chupacabra, but I'm warning you Spike gave me pointers. You're going down," she said, giving him a thumbs down.

"Pointers with what? His chin?" Reginald snidely remarked.

A fist pumped the air in victory while the other two gazed in shock. Daniel beamed cutely in pride. Falling to his hands and knees, Reginald appeared to be on the verge of an existential crisis. Somehow Daniel had beaten him by a singular point.

"I demand a rematch!" the red head cried in desperation.

"I won. Just accept it."

"I still lost. Why can't I win?" Mel sulked, staring at her empty hands.

At dawn, Johnathan entered the training hall, dragging his feet. There were dark shadows under his eyes and he looked like a broken man. Seeing him so defeated, Mel scrambled off the cold floor to his side. He opened his mouth and closed it, as if mulling over what he would say.

"Lord Lupus has decided that you will accompany us to the council. He has put his foot down on the matter and refuses to be swayed." He sighed, pacing the long room, inspecting the different weapons that lined the walls. "Because of this, I'm going to put you through hell these next few weeks. Infighting is forbidden during the council, but you'd look like an easy target. I'd like you to be able to fight a little better just in case the need would arise. Tsume will oversee your sparring for the next few days."

Mel watched the red head as they circled one another. She had lost count of what match they were on or who had the winning count. To her annoyance, Reginald had started to catch on to her small tricks to win the advantage but she still had one ace up her sleeve. They parried, stabbed, and danced in a swirl of wooden blades. Bruises lightly appeared as they dueled.

Mel dove, tossing the practice sword over her shoulder in a feint of a downward swing. Her punch was knocked to the side, sending her tottering over her feet. Regaining her balance, she smashed her heel into Reginald's hand, causing his sword to clatter across the floor. Her heel stung from the impact. Digging her feet in, she threw another punch. He caught her wrists, first one then the other.

"Can't keep using the same cheap tricks." Reginald smiled but it turned to a grimace as pain shot through his wrists when he tried to release her.

Mel gave a twisted grin at his look of bewilderment, digging her fingers into his wrists just like she had read about days ago. "Joint lock," she sang, teasing. Throwing her head back, bashing her forehead into his face. Pain exploded as she fell to her knees, gripping her throbbing head.

"Regret," she wheezed out, tears dripping from her eyes.

Peeking through blurry eyes, Mel spotted Reginald rolling and cursing. She debated apologizing but thought better of it. She wouldn't even accept one from herself at the moment. An apology would only make him angrier. He snarled, then leapt at her, sinking his nails into her arms. The two started rolling on the hard floor, screaming, clawing, and biting. Angry red lines appeared on arms and faces as the sparring match devolved into a full blown cat fight.

Mel climbed on top of him, ready to claw his face. A strong grip on the back of her neck yanked her off, sending her sprawling across the floor. Rolling onto her feet she lunged at the new assailant. The wind was knocked out of her lungs and throat, sending her into a coughing fit.

Tsume glared at her as she pinned Reginald to the floor with her knee. He was flailing vainly to escape her grip. The fight left him as he slumped into a puddle of seething rage.

"That's enough, you two. Go cool off. And if you dare try this crap again; I'll join in and things other than egos will be broken," she snapped, releasing the poor boy.

Defeated, the two dragged their feet down the hall. Silence lingered as they glared at each other.

"You just can't fight fair can you," Reginald hissed.

"I refuse to lose to you," Mel glared back. "This isn't over."

"Agreed."

Chapter 28

- -

Mel stood in front of the stable's wooden fence whistling a small tune as the horses stood about in the green pasture. A crisp breeze blew through her hair, making her shiver. The rays of dawn lit the dark sky, turning it a light pinkish orange. Savannah stuck her head out of the small brown bag next to Mel, yawned, tucking herself back inside. The soft click of footsteps announced the arrival of the others, making her cut the tune short.

The group stood in a small circle. Tsume, Johnathan, Cornelia, and Lupus carried small bags while Reginald and Kiba shot nervous glances at Tsume. The pattering of feet announced Daniel as he sprinted to the group panting.

"Since we are all here, are we ready," Lupus stated, rubbing his hands together. "Everyone knows what they will do."

"Reginald and I will be in charge of the defense of the village," Kiba said, shooting another glance at his wife. "No disrespect, but I think Tsume should stay. We know how she can be."

"Don't be like that, honey, it was already decided. I'm little Melosia's babysitter and that is that." Tsume hummed, throwing an arm around the girl, making her stumble.

"Here is a list of duties I've compiled." Johnathan handed over a thick parcel of papers to Reginald who looked like he was one cloud nine. "And despite her shortcomings, Tsume's strength is not something you can dispute."

"That's right, if anyone messes with my little girl, they'll have to answer to these weapons of mass destruction," she chimed in, raising her fists. Her husband buried his face in his hands, releasing a long groan. "Don't be like that," she snapped, smacking his back.

"If we are all set, let's head off; it's a long ride to our destination," Johnathan said, pulling up onto his spotted mare.

The journey took two long days of riding to complete. The group headed south of the village, riding next to the large mountain chain that seemed to run down the terrain for an eternity. Every now and then, they passed a small village or town, but the group didn't stop. They were surrounded by thick forest, although every so often they saw streams or meadows.

A loud rumble cut through the air as they rode up to a large lake at the foot of a mountain. A waterfall crashed down from its side, sending ripples of misty rainbows in the evening light. They stopped to let the horses drink from the icy clear water. The water was so clear you could see trout and other fish swimming under the surface.

Riding around the lake brought them to a large town at sunset. They dropped the horses off at the stable near the entrance of town and walked through the busy streets. Buildings at least two stories high, were painted in various colors that were accented by the banners they waved in front. The road was paved with gray stones, worn smooth from use. A building of dark stone sat in the middle of town.

Multiple banners flew along its columns. It was too far to make out the symbols emblazoned upon them. Torches lined the awning casting light around it like a beacon.

Finally, Lupus stopped in front of an inn, its red walls and gray banner were a welcome sight for the travelers. The words SCARLET TROUT INN shone in glowing floss woven into the banner along with the image of a fish. The group entered the inn and were met by the warmth of a fire and two large tables. Lupus walked to the owner, chatted him up, and came back with two brass keys.

"Upstairs," was all he said as he walked up the wooden staircase that creaked with every other step. After opening his door, he tossed the other key to Cornelia.

Once Cornelia opened the door, Tsume and Mel crashed onto the soft, feathery beds. They released a groan of relief in unison. Cornelia shook her head, taking a seat on the third bed that was next to the window, and gazed out into the streets beneath. A soft knock came at the door and it creaked open.

"I know you're all tired, but I brought some honey roasted hog and some bread." Lupus grinned, placing the trays down. "Also a message from Johnathan. He said, quote, 'tomorrow during the meeting, you two better not leave this room or cause trouble.' Don't kill the messenger. Goodnight," he added quickly before shutting the door.

"I can't believe him. Letting you come, only to be cooped up," Tsume whined the next morning. She stared intently at her hand of cards. She grinned toothily, throwing down the winning hand.

"Why can't I ever win, anything?" Mel questioned, looking at Savannah who was stretching in the sunlight.

"Maybe you overthink it or you're too strung up about winning." Tsume shrugged. She whined loudly again and threw herself to the floor.

"Johnathan only said today. It's not like it will be every day," Mel said, picking up the red cards and shuffling them for another round.

"Well, I don't want to wait for tomorrow, and I am older than him," Tsume exclaimed, jumping up to her feet. "Come on, I'm hungry."

"But we just ate roast beef sandwiches."

"Live a little. It'll be fun. I'm an adult, what could go wrong?"

Mel didn't think this was a great idea as she stared at the flock of geese honking and waddling on the outskirts of the town. Tsume and Savannah eyed the poultry eagerly, to Mel's discomfort. Of the few things Mel knew in this life, one was that geese were creatures of evil and not to be trifled with. She attempted to protest again, but was silenced by a wave of Tsume's hand.

"Don't worry. I'm just going to grab an egg or two. The fresher the better and it's free," she said. She climbed nimbly over the fence, snuck to the nest, and scooped up two large eggs. She turned smiling at Mel, but was confused when she saw the girl and cat start running toward a field of corn in panic. The rustling of feathers and shrill honking made Tsume turn her head. Then she ran, leaping over the fence as a wave of fifty geese angrily hissed and charged behind her.

She chucked the eggs over her shoulder, shattering them. "Take your dang eggs! Mel, get back here and help me!" she yelled, diving into the corn field after her.

Johnathan stood outside a small food stall with his friends going over some small details of the meeting.

"I wonder what Mel and Tsume are up to. Probably nothing good." Dj snickered.

"Don't worry I gave them strict orders to stay put for the day and rest," Johnathan replied, though he frowned with a small crease forming on his forehead.

"Look there they are," Daniel said, waving before raising an eyebrow. "Why are they running?"

The girls ran their boots skidding across the cobblestone unable to gain purchase as they turned. They scrambled past the boys with a glance, only shouting incoherently.

"What the actual hell?" Spike placed a hand on his hip.

"They said the geese are coming," Dj replied, cocking his head to the side, smiling.

"What's that supposed to mean? The geese are coming," Daniel smiled, then turned pale and ran after Mel and Tsume, shouting as well. "The geese are coming!"

The others looked and saw a wave of angry fowl descending upon them honking and hissing. Their mouths wide open, ready to bite anything in their way as their feathers puffed up. The boys and others on the street scattered. Spike easily took the lead leaving the others behind. Dj screamed as he tripped and the geese descended, swarming over his body as he reached out for help. Johnathan didn't look back.

Chapter 29

Mel dashed through an alley, she had lost sight of Tsume and the others. She hoped they had escaped. A glance over her shoulder confirmed she had escaped at least. She collided with someone, slamming onto the ground. Savannah went sprawling from her perch upon Mel's head. Glancing up to apologize, her throat constricted at the way this stranger's eyes glowered at her. The older teen stared at her like she was something lowlier than an insect to be trodden on.

"So...sorry about that," she fumbled, standing to dust herself off.

The man continued to glare at her, slicking his blonde hair back before speaking in a tone that made her bite her tongue. "I shouldn't expect much from the scum that lives here. At least your parents had the decency to teach you some form of manners."

"I said I was sorry," she said again, raising her head as Savannah curled around her ankle.

"And for that I complimented you, or would you rather I punish you for an attack on my person," he said. A strange glint within his eyes as if it thrilled him to fight.

Mel's heart hammered as her body froze up. Something wasn't right about this guy. The way he looked at her and expressed himself made it clear that he believed she was beneath him. He almost seemed like he was trying to provoke her into fighting him. A glance at her feet showed Savannah felt the same; her pointed teeth were bared, her hair stood on end, and her tail lashed back and forth.

"At least you have a cat; if it were anything else, I might have to kill it to teach you a lesson in picking fights with those above you," he stated flatly, like he was speaking about the weather.

Mel's voice failed her; how was she supposed to respond to that? What kind of sick person would ever say something that twisted? She felt dirty standing near him. The call of her name was like the sound of heaven's bells. Spinning on her heels, she waved to Tsume, thankful to be saved from this stranger. A wary glance over her shoulder made her sigh in relief, he had vanished.

"There you are, Mel. We did it, we're dead. Even if you're old man Lupus' niece, John's going to have our hides. Maybe if we come up with a plausible excuse, we can make it...What's wrong? You're pale, noone tried to pick a fight with you did they," Tsume questioned, reaching over to pat Mel on the head. She scanned the road warily.

"It's nothing. I'm just a little winded. Let's go get that tongue lashing from Johnathan over with. Maybe Uncle will save us from the worst of it." She pushed Tsume's hand away along with the encounter from her head.

They entered their room with heads hung low, an attempt to appear sullen and defeated, Johnathan stood in the center with arms crossed, a deep frown watches into his pretty features. Mel took a deep breath, ready to speak about what she had practiced on the way.

"It's Tsume's fault! It was her idea. It was all her idea! I told her not to, but she wouldn't listen to me. I'm the victim here!"

Tsume tossed her head in shock. "You little...I thought we were friends!"

"We are, but I don't want to die for you!"

"You better sleep with an eye open for this, you little snitch!"

"I'm too young to die over something you did!"

"I have children!"

"You've lived long enough, then!"

"Enough! I don't care whose fault it is or was. Sit now!"

An hour later. Mel's ankles and feet cramped up from sitting on them. Tsume looked to be in the same boat. They both looked down on their knees as Johnathan ranted about responsibility and being respectable.

"And you know we had to apologize to the goose farmer. Dj says he might never be about to eat bird meat again. Finally, I gave you two, one simple order and you couldn't even follow it," he ranted. He took a deep breath and exhaled it. "You're both going to sleep without dinner goodnight." He stormed out of the room.

Johnathan had decided that one night without food was enough of a punishment and that keeping the duo locked up might have them act out more. As an act of mercy he has allowed them to leave the inn as long as Daniel or another responsible adult was present. Mel stared at the stage that was in the middle of the town's commons area. She squatted to the side of the commons that seemed to get more crowded as time passed, playing with Savannah as Tsume stood beside her, arms crossed, a deep frown etched into her face.

"Why only after lunch," Mel asked after a moment of thought.

"Because that is when most of the important meeting stuff ends and the second in commands and in turn Daniel can leave. Meaning we will have a babysitter," Tsume sulked, flopping onto the ground.

"You did make a scene and scared Dj off poultry," Mel muttered, tossing a small ball for the kitten to chase.

"Shut up, traitor. I can't believe you threw me to the wolves."

"Like I said, I don't want to die for you; no offense."

"Offense taken, you made that clear last night."

"Sorry, Tsume. You're still my knight in shining armor for saving me from that snake."

"Don't try and butter me up," she replied, turning her back.

Mel smiled, throwing her arms around Tsume's neck in a hug. "I love you. Mi amor."

"John said you two were being prickly with each other but I see you're alright," Dj said, walking up with a wave, a young girl trailing behind. She wore an embroidered dress with a tan vest. Her black hair was pulled into two buns with draping braids. Her pink eyes gleamed as she skipped.

The girl ran to Mel and gripped her hands in her smaller ones. "Hello, I'm March, Dj's little sister. I hope we can be friends."

"I hope so too." Mel examined the girl looking for resemblances. "And I'll say it again, it's hard to believe you have sisters Dj."

"It's hard especially when you have a twin," Dj shrugged.

"Dj. Don't run off with your sister," an older man snapped. He had glasses, green eyes, and the same black hair as the two siblings.

"Sorry, Pops. March wanted to meet Mel," he replied, then pointed at the man. "Mel, this is my old man, Draco. Pops, this is Melosia, old man Lupus' niece."

"I know, Lupus informed me earlier. Thank you for looking after my son. He can be difficult, and I wish he would take things more seriously."

"Sorry Pops, I'm not Valentina," Dj said. "Too bad she's too hot blooded for the job so you're stuck with me."

Draco stared at his son before turning to his daughter. "March, the dance will start soon. Come along."

"Yes, father," she sang as she bounced toward the stage.

Mel watched as different women gathered around the stage in various dancing outfits. She saw Cornelia was a part of the dancer group, and she was talking to a woman with mint colored hair in braids and a scarf over her face. Mel shot a glance at Dj and Tsume. "I'd hate to sound stupid but what dance is going to happen."

"The dance of the elementalists. It's tradition to make sure the weather is good for the upcoming seasons," Tsume explained.

"They dance to appease the spirits of nature. It's said if they miss a dance even once, nature devastates the land," Dj said darkly, then yelped as Tsume smacked the back of his head.

The steady beat of drums filled the air, accompanied by strings, bells, and flutes. The dancers moved like a wave, fluid as one. They spun and leapt across the stage. Stomping in time with the beat of the drums as it hit a crescendo and accelerated. At the end of the dance, the women bowed as one and the crowd roared in applause.

The dances continued for a little longer, four more dances with solo dancers. Mel felt tired just watching the grace, skill, and speed at which the dancers moved. A part of her somewhat wanted to dance with them to the beat of music. After it ended and the crowd was dispersing, Dj left with his sister and Cornelia walked to Mel with the mint haired dancer in tow, holding her hand.

"Did you enjoy the dance?" Cornelia asked, as Mel and Tsume rose to greet her.

"Yes, it was beautiful. Would you teach me some of the steps," Mel asked. Taking a glance at the new woman, she saw that the silk beaded scarf covered her eyes. She wore a dancer's outfit like Cornelia except with yellow accents.

"I will for our next lesson. This is Cecily, my friend. We are going to have tea at the inn. Will you accompany us?" Cornelia asked.

Chapter 30

The group of women sat on the floor of their room with a small basket of pastries that they bought along the way and a kettle of tea. Cornelia and Cecily were chatting as Mel ate a small moist cake topped with a lemon frosting. Tsume laid on her side, snacking on cookies and tossing bits to Savannah.

Mel kept sneaking glances at Cecily's face. The scarf around her eyes appeared pretty thick and hard to see through. She reached out pale hands, rubbing her thumb on her silver tea cup. Cornelia caught Mel's eyes and the girl turned her head, feeling her face heat up.

"Are you interested in Cecily's scarf?" Cornelia asked, picking up a small cookie.

"Yes," she replied, sitting up straighter.

Cecily smiled, bringing her hands up to her head. She unfolded the scarf, putting it down onto her knees. Mel's stomach twisted and her voice failed her. Where Cecily's eyes should have been was a ragged scar cut across her face. "Quite ghastly, isn't it?" she said with a weary grin.

Mel struggled with her words, not wanting to put her foot in her mouth. In the end, she nodded and flushed again. "Sorry. Um yes, what happened?"

"There is nothing to apologize for. When I was a very young girl, a cruel rumor had started to circulate that if you blinded an elementalist they would be able to see the future clearly. Many gifted young girls were snatched from their villages and homes; never by their own tribes though," she said, swirling her cup of tea. The cooling tea ran down her fingers like dark tears.

"That's awful!" Mel gasped, touching her own eyes.

"It isn't done anymore. This place used to be much crueler, but that is in the past now. Good came out of that horrible situation, though. My Lady Cynthia became friends with your uncle, but through the ordeal I met my Cornelia, my most treasured companion," she said, taking Cornelia's dark hands into her own. She gave them a gentle squeeze, a soft smile graced her face. "It was terribly scary, but I wouldn't change what happened. The past is what shapes us into the people we are today and we must look toward the future."

Silence settled over the room for some time before the two dancers began happily chatting again. Tsume rolled onto her side toward Mel as she pouted, deep in thought. A sly smile crossed her face after a few moments. "Hey, Mel, there's a festival tomorrow night. Are you going to be with Daniel?"

"Yeah, Dj told me about it. We're all going," she replied, excited. "Why? You're coming with us."

Tsume pouted again, closing her eyes and sitting up. She brought her hand to her chin and turned her head to the side. "But wouldn't you prefer if it was just you with Daniel?"

Mel knew where this was going. She sighed, turning her head away as she felt a small warmth on her cheeks. "It's not like that. We are friends," she muttered as Tsume giggled, rolling on her back. She continued to tease Mel.

A small knock kept Mel from throttling her in embarrassment at the harassment. Johnathan popped his head through the door. "Mel, Lord Lupus would like you to come and greet his friends."

"My uncle has friends?" she gasped, covering her mouth, causing him to roll his eyes. "Coming," she added, quickly getting up and shooting a glare at Tsume who winked.

Mel followed Johnathan into the next room where her uncle sat with two others. One was Draco, Dj's father, and the other was a woman. The woman had blond hair held in a ponytail, piercing blue eyes, and sharp features vaguely familiar to someone she knew. Lupus nodded as they walked in and stretched out his arms. "This is my niece, Melosia."

"I know, I met her earlier today," Draco stated, uninterested.

"I am Cynthia, Spike's mother," the woman said with a small nod.

"You two are no fun," Lupus groaned, slumping back down and scrunching up his face. "I guess if you two don't want to marvel at my own flesh and blood, she can leave."

"What?" Mel asked, making a similar face of confused displeasure.

"I just wanted to introduce you to my old friends. That's all," he said, sending a pointed glance at Draco.

"He just called on you to show you off. Ridiculous." Daniel snorted, covering his mouth with the back of his hand as the duo walked up to the others the next day. Mel shoved him playfully in retaliation for teasing her as Savannah scampered off ahead.

The town's commons area had transformed to a brightly decorated celebration. Stalls with games, food, and gifts stood in neat lines crammed together, side by side. Lanterns were strung about the area dangling like fruits from a vine. The aroma of food stalls filled the air along with the sound of laughter and cheer.

They explored the stall games. Spike dominated, throwing knives at targets. Tsume and Dj broke the strength testing games, much to the screaming frustration of its owner who yelled something about the fifth time today. Johnathan made ring toss look like a lost art form. Daniel was decent at everything he did. The only thing Mel won, much to her own displeasure, was a meat-ball eating contest. The group kept giving the prizes that they won to Mel to hold, only adding to her resentment.

She caught Daniel staring for a brief second. He paused, then grabbed her hand, dragging her to a small tightrope game. He smiled, pointing at the pair of thin ropes that hung over a small pit of hay. She agreed with a nod and the two squared off, one on each rope. He playfully gave her a thumbs down while she drew her finger across her neck. They took off. He swayed but kept his balance to the halfway point before diving unceremoniously into the hay. She swayed a little before straightening completely and with amazing grace, walked the rope in seconds, hopping off at the end. She punched the air playfully, jumping up and down in glee at the victory.

Mel stopped, feeling a chill creep down her spine. It felt like eyes were peering at her. Turning she scanned the milling crowd. Nothing seemed suspicious. Daniel tapped her shoulder and she shook her head to chase off the tingling feeling that lingered on her skin.

As the sun set, painting the sky in vibrant colors, the group sat on the roof of the inn, staring up at the darkening sky. A loud crack and boom echoed into the dark night as bright sparks exploded in the sky. The fireworks blazed through the sky, lighting it up as they watched.

Mel took her eyes off the beautiful lights to look at her side. The lights lit up Daniel's face, his brown eyes reflecting the light show. She felt a small clutch in her chest. Their eyes met and she looked back at the sky, her heart beating rapidly, thumping in her ears. He reached over and grabbed her hand dragging her to her feet, a large grin on his face as he spun her around. They stumbled and swayed. Her laughter echoed in the night as she danced with him on the tiled roof.

Taking their lead, Tsume grabbed Johnathan against his will, dragging him around. Dj took his little sister by the hands, tossing her into the air and spinning her around. Spike chuckled with his mother as Lupus and Draco shared a drink. The festivities lasted long into the night and Mel felt like she wouldn't have changed anything about it.

Chapter 31

It was the last day of the council as Mel and Tsume stared up at the white fluffy clouds. Against the clear blue of the sky, the clouds appeared close enough to touch. Mel reached up for one as Tsume laughed at her childish behavior.

"It looks like a fox," Mel said, still reaching.

"I don't see it. Looks more like Savannah," Tsume teased, elbowing her in the side while the kitten laid on her chest. "Last day and no problems."

"Is that excluding the geese because if my memory is correct. That was problematic." She grinned at Tsume. "Dj died. We'll never see his beautiful face again."

"Let it go," Tsume whined with a grin that slipped when she saw Johnathan walking their way. She waved, tilting her head. "What are you doing out early?"

"Victor has called Melosia to be presented before the council," Johnathan said, his eyebrows furrowed and his tone on edge.

Tsume cursed, running her hands over her head. "Out of all the people to find out it had to be him. There won't be a problem, will there?" she said, clenching her fists.

"Like we said before, there's nothing to worry about since she is Lupus' niece," he said, turning his head to the side.

"But still; it's Victor. He'll do anything to cause a scene. Whenever there's drama or a disappearance during the council, he's normally at the center of it." She growled and raised her chin. "Let me come."

"No, just Mel. If you come, he might try and make things more difficult. This will be a simple ritual of officially letting her join the tribes. Nothing to fear," he said, giving Mel's shoulder a gentle squeeze. He led her away. Jonathan was always the picture of composure, yet something in his clipped tone had her bite her lip. He was uncertain and worried; she could tell and it made her tense.

They climbed up the stone steps into the dark large building, its multiple banners flapping in the crisp autumn breeze. Mel felt a chill, entering the building and going down a narrow halfway into a large room as the torches danced casting long shadows.

The room was lit only by the candles that lined the wall and a singular candelabra that sat on the large circular table where thirteen occupants with various hair color and skin tones sat. Embroidered banners dangled behind each chair, showing a golden hourglass, yin and yang, silver fleur de lis, green tree, silver cross bones, red skull with long fangs, black raven, brown paw print with claws, orange flowers on a stalk, and a green snake eating its tail. Mel took her place behind her uncle. Johnathan kept a hand on her shoulder. To her right stood Spike who gave a stiff nod and on her left stood Dj who gave a cheeky grin.

The man that sat ahead had blond hair and slightly familiar green eyes, and behind him stood the man Mel had run into at the beginning of the week. "Is that Victor?" she whispered to her uncle who nodded.

A chill crept down her spin at the twisted smile that graced Victor's face. He leaned down and whispered in the man's ear who then nodded and rose. "Lupus, I'm surprised you brought your niece to town without introducing her to us. I'm shocked to even learn you had a family. To keep such a secret, given how conceited you can be," he purred.

"Now, now, Julius, no need to be like that. You see, Melosia is still in the midst of her training and I would prefer to show her off when that is complete," Lupus replied, leaning onto the table.

"But why, Lupus? She is adorable; makes me want to eat her up," a ginger woman said her eyes sparkled with mirth.

"I don't see the problem if she can fight," a large dark skinned man with tattoos said. While a younger man nodded in agreement, the fire light casting shadows on his scarred face.

"I'm just curious as to where she has been this whole time," Julius said, spreading his hands out. "Like I said earlier, I thought you had no family."

"My niece was with her mother, I just recently collected her," Lupus explained, leaning back.

"She is from the other world, I'm guessing? I heard a rumor long ago that you had a brother that fled there," a dark woman with sharp eyes and red hair stated, with the indifference of talking about the weather.

"As perceptive as always, Evita," Lupus replied as the room seemed to stiffen.

"But isn't that against our most ancient codes? Jumping between dimensions is something only a demon should do and not be abused by the elementalist," Julius stated, a grin on his face.

"Exactly," said Victor. "Father, I think the wolf tribe should be punished for this. Lord Lupus has always done things as he pleases; it's about time he learned his place. Let's execute her, it might be a little drastic, but it would solve the problem." He was not masking his contempt at all.

"We all know we don't follow as many of the old codes as we used to. Do we wear silly masks to these meetings? No. Do we kidnap and blind young girls? No. I could go on. An execution would be going way too far!" Cynthia snapped, waving her hand furiously.

"I agree with Lady Cynthia on this matter. The wolves have done nothing wrong. The squirrel tribe will support them as they have us," a small woman squeaked out.

"Ligeia, silly girl, you should pick your battles better. As you can see, the only ones that truly want the wolves to burn are the saber tooth and panther tribes, though if something happened, there would be a rift in the council's balance," Evita said, talking down to the poor girl like someone would to a small child.

More arguments broke out. Mel's head hurt from trying to keep up with the conversations and to keep people's names straight. But what Evita said seemed to ring true. Most everyone was ranting about not caring about the dimension hopping at all. Mel noticed that Draco remained silent through the ordeal, slowly tapping a fingernail on the table. A loud screech screamed as his chair's feet scraped across the tiled floor.

"I think I've had enough of this farce. You want to mess with the girl. Let's put it to a vote for induction to the tribes or banishment.

There is an odd number here," Draco's voice boomed bringing the room to silence.

"But that would include Daniel, and one person cannot be considered a tribe," Victor said.

"I see you have eyes Victor, but why don't you use them. The vote would be a draw if Daniel weren't included. We all know how the council is divided. The bear, tiger, panther, griffin, weasel, and saber tooth stand as one. As do the hyena, badger, cheetah, dragon, squirrel, and wolf support one another. Let the coyote boy vote. It keeps it from being a stalemate," Draco explained as his son nodded giving a thumbs up to Daniel who tried to hide his face.

"That trash shouldn't even be considered a person, let alone a tribe. A coward's vote is not needed and he will only vote with the wolves, making you win!" Victor sneered, slamming a hand on the table.

"You scum. What right do you have to mock him? He is worth more than a sick freak like you!" Spike growled. His mother put a hand up to silence him.

"Let it go. Julius control your son and keep your petty rivalry with the wolves out of our politics. Admit it, you have lost this battle," she said, closing her eyes. "Or do you have more complaints?"

Johnathan cleared his throat loudly, bringing all eyes on him. "If you would allow me to speak? We have a tournament every few years. Melosia is under my tutelage and will be more than able to show her worth to the tribes. Have her fight in the tournament to prove her strength."

A silence settled as many of the leaders nodded in agreement. A vote was held. Six hands rose to exile while seven rose to induct. Mel was safe, but it also meant she would have to prove herself in a tournament. She didn't know if she should be relieved or anxious. Her head felt light.

The meeting was adjourned and they went into the inn. Lupus told everyone to pack their things. In a rush, the group was on their horses, headed home. Mel's head spun from all that had transpired. She couldn't stop thinking about fighting in a tournament. If the leaders in the room showed up, what would happen? She didn't want to fight anyone there; they looked way too strong. She could barely breath from the dust the horses kicked up. They had left so quickly to head back to Stella Luna that she didn't get to say bye to Spike or Dj.

"Why are we in such a rush?" Mel asked Tsume, the only one in their small group that didn't appear ready to snap under the pressuring silence.

Tsume turned, a grim expression on her lovely face. She seemed to be thinking over what to say. "Victor lost in that little power play. He'll be livid; he's used to getting what he wants," she paused, licking her lips in thought. "He's not right in the head, I think. He wants violence. Every council, he tried something to start a fight and being the son of the leader of his tribe makes him untouchable."

Mel's skin tingled, getting covered in goosebumps. She remembered the way he looked at her during the meeting, like she was an insect to be dissected. And how he threatened to kill Savannah just because she bumped into him. How he wanted to kill her for existing. Mel's stomach turned. *I won't ever see him again*, she thought, praying that would be the truth.

Chapter 32

The days passed by in an eerie calm. The kind of calm that made you jumpy for no reason; it just put you on edge. Johnathan let Mel off from training for her to clear her mind from the last few days before training would ramp up again. With nothing else better to do during the day, she sat in her room, reading, while at night her dreams were plagued by monsters dancing around her with red eyes. The monsters would transform into beasts with long fangs that would try and devour her as she ran.

She lay in bed with the sheer fabric of the canopy pulled to the side. She thumbed through the book of fables her uncle had given her. Kicking her feet in the air, she leaned her chin in one hand as she scanned the lines of the children's story. It was about a maiden who wished to marry a prince; she went on a journey to save the prince with her best friend and along the way she realized the one she loved had been by her side the entire time.

Mel snapped the book shut. She knew it would end like that; those kinds of stories usually did. The main character would pine for someone out of their league and eventually figure out it was the friend they loved. A glimpse of Daniel flittered through her mind; she flushed, smashing her face into the plush pillows of her bed. She cursed softly. Ever since the festival maybe even before that a strange feeling haunted her at the thought of the boy. His kind smile, his warm eyes, his honest personality, and he was her friend, a most precious friend. He was someone she cherished and cared for. Grimacing, she rolled on her bed, flailing her legs about. *I don't like him in that way*, she thought over and over again. Yet the flutter of her heart told her differently. At some point she'd stopped thinking of him as a friend and began thinking of him as something else, but what, she couldn't pin down.

Sighing, she sat up, grabbing a pen and some paper. She was going to nip this in the bud now, she decided. Scribbling on the paper, a frown grew. She crumbled the parchment and tossed it to the side of the room. She tried again as Savannah played with the slowly increasing balls of paper that littered the floor. Burrowing her warm face into her hands, she groaned. What did she even want to write? She barely understood how she felt. She walked over to the silver mirror on her dresser.

She ran her fingers over the floral design; the cold metal felt nice as she pressed it to her cheek. Opening it, she gazed at herself in its reflective surface, a small smile tugged at her lips. "Daniel gave this to me the first time we met," she said to Savannah, bringing the mirror to her chest, Savannah stopped chasing a paper ball to look at her master.

An idea popped into Mel's head as she jumped on her bed, picking up the pen again. "Daniel, I've been thinking about some things since the council, and I'd like to talk to you about them. Can you think of anywhere I haven't seen yet, great tour guide?" she said as she scribbled the note down. She called for Savannah; the kitten took the letter between her sharp fangs. "Take this to Daniel," she said, and the kitten nodded, scurrying off to deliver the message.

Mel fell back on her bed, placing the book of fables on her face after rereading the same line multiple times. Waiting for Savannah to return felt like an eternity. When she finally returned and scratched at the door, Mel jumped up, took the letter from her, and petted her affectionately around the ears. She took a deep breath before opening the folded note. "*I have something I'd like to talk about as well. I know just the place. Meet me tomorrow morning before the sun rises at the front gates of the village.*"

A strange giddy feeling bubbled inside her as she tried to go to sleep. She wouldn't say she liked the feeling but she wouldn't say she hated it either. She made a pile of pillows and buried her face in them, finally drifting off to sleep.

The forest air was crisp. The small puffs of her breath could be seen lingering and floating up into the air like will-o-wisps as the duo walked through the dark woods. Daniel smiled, holding a lantern as he led Mel deeper into the wilderness. They had to be out of the borders of the village, she thought, as the predawn light started to filter through the leaves that rustled with every icy breeze. The song of birds was slowly swelling as Mel and Daniel walked further. Savannah's ears perked up, twitching with interest at every small disturbance of the underbrush.

"Here we are. Right through here," Daniel announced, pulling back a thick branch for her to walk past.

Mel entered the clearing, and her boots clanked on stone. She gazed in wonder at the stone ruins that loomed around her, crumbling and old, but still standing. Trailing her fingers along the gritty edges, she felt faded symbols carved into the surface.

"Over here," Daniel called, patting the floor where he sat in the dead center of the small ruins.

The two sat and watched as the sun rose. The dawn's rays filtered through the trees like spotlights onto the stones around them. The beams appeared to reflect and bounce off the white stone, making the area glow with an unnatural light. It was like a mystical forest for fairies. Mel watched in wonder, not able to speak as the world glowed and sparkled around her in a spell of unnatural beauty.

The light glistened red and gold. The visible beams of light that almost seemed to dance lingered with an ethereal light. Even Savannah, who was almost always moving and would normally chase the sparkles, sat transfixed by the spectacle.

"It's beautiful, isn't it?" Daniel whispered, leaning close to her.

All Mel could do was nod in agreement. She felt something brush against her fingers. Glancing down, she saw it was his hand. They intertwined their fingers in a warm, shy embrace. A small blush covered both of their faces as they watched the lights of the sun-rise wash over the stones.

"Melosia," Daniel said, looking her seriously in the eyes and giving her hand a nervous squeeze, "I wanted...I've wanted to tell you something. I bet you've figured it out already but I...I mean.."

He stopped cocking his head to the side, thinking of the best way to say it. He smiled sheepishly, leaning forward. His warm breath was on her face as they leaned closer, hearts pounding. It seemed no words needed to be said as their lips almost touched.

"Well, would you look at what we have here? A wolf and a coyote a little too far from the safety of their den it would be a shame if something dangerous would appear," a voice sneered, shattering the peace and spell of the morning's calm.

Mel and Daniel pulled apart, staring at the shadows at the edge of the ruins. The man stalked out of the dark shadows, a crooked smile on his face. His green eyes gleamed with a twisted light. He absentmindedly stroked the hilt of his sword on his hip. Mel felt the world shift under her as fear chilled through her veins like a frozen river in winter. This man was dangerous. After all, he wanted her dead.

Chapter 33

Lupus sat at his desk, flipping through some documents while Johnathan stood off to the side, filing some of the work he had completed. The older man stretched and yawned. Everything at the council had gone fine, so he should be relaxed, but something felt wrong in the back of his mind. An anxious feeling stayed bubbling inside as he tapped the pen on the table, Johnathan shot an irritable look in his direction.

"What is it?" he asked after Lupus released another sigh.

Lupus leaned back in his chair, placing his hands onto his lap. "I have a bad feeling things went too well. Julius is one thing; he does what he thinks is right and likes to antagonize us. But his son, Victor, never makes things easy. After the vote he stayed silent. Normally, he would have continued to throw a fit or make demeaning comments, but he didn't."

"Maybe he finally learned to keep his mouth shut when he's lost," Johnathan replied, placing a few papers on the large wooden desk.

"I've given Mel the last few days off to relax and from what I've seen, she's cooped herself up in her room, safe."

Lupus tapped his pen again before nodding. "I think it's best if she doesn't leave the village at all for the next month at least."

Johnathan paused to look him over, then sighed. "Very well I'll inform her during breakfast to stay indoors. She'd enjoy that."

The sound of heels on wood echoed through the halls outside breaking the calm. They looked at each other, then the door as it flew open. Cornelia was in disarray, her wavy white hair puffed up and frizzled on end like she'd just woken from a night-mare. She was out of breath, yet kept trying to speak, shaking her hands, frantically making motions as she gasped for air.

Lupus was by her side in a second. He held her shoulders in a comforting embrace. Concern was evident in his dark eyes as he squeezed her shoulders, looking her over. "What is it Cornelia? Breath, slowly."

"A nightmare or a vision. I went to Melosia's room but she was not there. She is not in the mansion. It is a blood red dawn, blood will be spilt, and I fear she is the one in danger. We have to find her," she finally spit out, tripping over the words, the green of her eyes flashing.

Lupus felt a spike of anxiety in his gut. Cornelia's sixth sense was always accurate. If she believed his niece was in danger, then she probably was. He had sworn to her mother that he would let nothing happen to her and he meant it. "Johnathan, get the others. We'll search through town. Have Tsume and Kiba both run a patrol of our borders," he ordered, turning to him.

They had all come out to the hall when the sound of shattering glass resonated in the air. The noise had come from the storage room where important items used to be kept. Lupus fiddled with the door knob. "Maybe Savannah is playing where she shouldn't be, and that is why you couldn't find Mel," he joked, hoping to find his niece and her cat with their hand in the cookie jar as he pushed the door open.

The torches that lined the walls lit up, casting their light upon the empty dusty room full of various items and relics. But not a living soul was in sight. Lupus' eyes fell upon the crystalline glass stand that held the black staff; the glass lay shattered upon the floor like crystals twinkling in the light. The staff stood straight up, its blade flashing wickedly in the light as it unhinged. An inky dark puddle of shadows swirled around the tip as the scythe sank through the stand disappearing as black sparks shot through the air.

"When did he make a contract?" Johnathan asked, cursing under his breath.

A feeling of cold dread replaced the fear in Lupus' stomach, and he had a possible revelation. "Forget the scythe! Mel is in danger and we have to find her!"

Mel's eyes lock with Victor's as she took a step back. Why was he here? What did he want? A hundred questions flew through her mind as her heart beat quickly in her ribcage almost like it wanted to escape. Savannah's fur bristled as she hissed. Daniel had gone bone pale, his eyes darted, searching for an escape route.

"No, no, no. You're not going back to that village, girl. You see I'm a little ticked about how that meeting went, and I want to have a nice conversation. You have two options: You can run away into the wilderness and die like a dog or we can go with my personal favorite; I kill you right now." He took a step closer and they took a step back. "You can't beat me in a fight or out-run me; so I'll give you a few seconds to decide."

Mel's eyes met Daniel's. They reached a silent agreement. The obvious choice was, they'd run for it. Her hands lingered at her waist, her fingers gripped the hidden knives at her side. She whipped her arm out, throwing the knives as they turned to run.

Victor didn't blink as he dodged the knives. He lurched after them. Savannah jumped out to intercept and he punted the kitten with a single kick into a tree. The sound of breaking bones and a shrill squeal echoed as the kitten crumpled to the floor.

The sound caused Mel to feel rage, fear, and nausea all at the same time. She spun on her heel, drawing another knife. He grabbed her wrist, twisting it as pain shot through her arm, making her release the blade. It clattered on the stone floor. A kick in the back of her legs made her fall to her knees. Pain exploded as they collided with the ground. She twisted and thrashed, trying to escape his vice grip.

Daniel scooped up a discarded knife and ran at Victor's back. Victor rolled his eyes, releasing her wrist. He grabbed Daniel's hand, yanking him forward, then elbowing him in the throat and drove his fist into his chin. A grin slipped across his face as he kneed Daniel in the stomach and threw him into a stone pillar. Then, picking up the knife, Victor slammed it into Daniel's hand, pinning him to the pillar.

"No!" Mel cried, as she stumbled, trying to get to her feet.

Daniel yanked at the knife, coughing up blood. He looked at Mel, desperation clear in his pained face. "Run," he pleaded between coughs.

Mel froze, her mind swimming. If she left Daniel, he'd get more hurt or worse, but if she didn't run, so would she. Could she even escape? She couldn't leave him. But what if she could get help? Her hair was grabbed roughly. She felt strands getting yanked from her scalp. Her head was slammed into the stone ground repeatedly and then grinded in. Blood filled her mouth from her bleeding nose. She spit out globs of it every time her head rose. Tears of pain and terror spilled out of her eyes, blending with the blood, giving it an iron and salt taste. Another knife was brought to her throat and pushed against it so that each shallow breath she took caused it to prick her skin.

Savannah snarled savagely, descending upon Victor, claws pulled out, fangs bared. The air felt metallic. A bright flash engulfed the kitten and she screamed in agony. Mel heard a resounding crack making her bones rattle. Savannah collapsed, thick acrid smoke billowing off her signed fur.

Mel saw red as flames erupted around her. Ripping herself from his startled grip, Mel scrambled away from her attacker and the dying flames. She felt the air change again and then a white light struck her. The pain was excruciating. It was like she was being electrocuted; the scream that ripped its way from her lungs left her throat raw as she collapsed. She lay on the ground, her body spasming in random jerks.

The sound of Victor's slow approach was deafeningly loud to her ears. The sound of him pulling the sword from its hilt made her want to vomit in terror as she tried to crawl, dragging her limp body forward. A foot slammed into the small of her back. The heel dug in painfully with a twist.

"I think I've played with you enough," he said, lifting his foot up.

Using the last of her draining strength, she spun onto her feet, ignoring the screaming pain. Snatching up her knife, she tried to defend herself against the sword that fell upon her. The knife shattered on impact. Her arm went numb from the power of the impact as the long sword cut into her forearm. An angry red gash poured blood as she cradled her right arm, scooting away in panic. Victor smiled, his teeth gleaming in the morning light as he stalked after her, clearly enjoying her terror.

Through the pain, she gritted her teeth and summoned fire again in a small ring around her. Victor paused, gazing at her pathetic defense as her blood pooled around her, sizzling in the flames. But then black sparks started to dance along her blood trail. Electric current stated to jump out of the blood and into the flames, making them erupt and turn to black, causing Victor to stop in his tracks. The black flames died out as a swirling mass of darkness appeared before her and the sparks seemed to absorb the rest of the blood. A black scythe emerged from the portal of darkness, its red tassels dangling from the hilt, swaying in the breeze. Mel knew this weapon. She saw it once before in another form under glass. Shakily, she reached her left hand for it, desperate for a weapon to defend herself.

Victor was in front of her, about to thrust his claymore down. A mixture of rage, contempt, and maybe even fear, flashed across his face. She wouldn't make it in time, and she was too weak to fight back anyway, so what was the point? She dropped her arm, the fight and drive to live gone, leaving her numb to the soul. Closing her eyes, she resigned herself to her death to come. The only sounds were the drumming of her beating heart and a gut wrenching scream of agony followed by a clang of metal.

Chapter 34

With her eyes screwed shut Mel waited for death again, yet it didn't come. She never felt the pain of the sword piercing through her body nor her life blood pour out. Was dying really this painless? Something warm and sticky was dripping onto her face, rolling down her cheeks like thick tears. Cracking open one eye, her world was shattered. Her scream died in her throat, only coming out in a strangled gasp.

The point of the sword had stopped inches from her face, covered and dripping with blood. Daniel's blood. He had stopped the sword from killing her by using his own body as a shield to protect her. Slowly, he turned his head and smiled at her, blood steadily dripping from his mouth like a stream. Victor grimaced, pushing him off the sword with his foot with a wet squelch.

Mel grabbed Daniel as he crumpled, and cradled him in her arms. She slammed her hand on the wound to his chest as his life blood poured out through her fingertips. She sobbed as the blood kept pouring. He coughed a mouthful of blood and tried to smile again, despite his pain.

"Mel, stop. It's okay. I want to tell you..." He stopped to cough and heave in rattled breaths.

"No, stop, save your strength," she replied, shaking, dread filling her as she desperately ripped her shirt to soak up the blood and stop the endless flow.

"You...we both know I'm a goner. I..I just want..ed to te..l you how I fel...eel." He struggled to speak as the blood kept coming up in waves.

"I know I...I know. I feel the same." Mel smiled at him as her tears poured out and pulled his injured hand to her face, cradling it as her throat and chest constricted with pain like no other. "So please, hang on."

"I'm .so.. gla..d...Melosia...mi..amor..." he said. A single tear rolled down his cheek. It gleamed as it went. A weak but peaceful smile grew on his face.

Daniel's eyes grew dull, and his hand went limp, slipping out of Mel's grip. Mel leaned over him, gently grabbing his shoulder. "Daniel. Daniel? Daniel, open your eyes. Oh please, don't die. Why did you do that! Please don't leave me! Don't die on me, Daniel!" she screamed out, sobs wrecking her body. Pulling him into her arms as she cried out, burying her face into his still warm neck. She begged and pleaded, rocking back and forth as he grew colder. Her voice cracked from the choking sobs that seemed to be strangling her from the inside out. It was getting harder and harder for her to breathe through the sobs and screams.

"Oh, look, he died," Victor said with such indifference it was almost like he stabbed her again. She wanted to fight back, to avenge Daniel, but her body wouldn't cooperate. She just sat there holding Daniel in her arms. Victor brought the side of the long sword to her face and tapped her with the flat of the blade, smearing the blood that coated it onto her cheek. He put the tip to her chin lifting her face to meet his bright eyes. "Look at me. That's a nice look, full of despair. You know it's your fault he's dead, right? If you never came here and met him, he wouldn't be dead. How does it feel to cause the death of someone you love?"

"No, you did it," she sobbed out. Her throat felt thick and swollen; breathing was getting harder by the second. Pain exploded as her head was thrown to the side from his back handed punch.

"Really? If you had stayed with your other life, would we be here right now? Oh, poor Mel all alone, holding onto the boy she killed. If she wasn't born, he'd still be here," he sang, grabbing her bangs, bringing her face closer to his. "Who will save her, nobody knows. She's all alone. What a pathetic little girl. Anyone near her is sure to get hurt. Who will she kill next? Her uncle, her cat? Or maybe she'll take her own life instead."

Victor kept on mercilessly taunting her, seeming to enjoy every cruel word that cut her to her soul. Her heart hurt, her body hurt, and her head hurt, but it didn't matter anymore. She wanted it to end. Every cruel word was true. It was all her fault, everything. Her vision started to darken as she blinked, the colors dissolving around her. Darkness overtook her.

Mel stood in a dark space, its expanse ever reaching. A black door with gold accents stood before her, a door she'd seen before in her dreams. She flung them open and ran through. She ran and ran, on and on through the darkness, trying to escape the pain and the sorrow.

"It's only a dream! It's not real!" she yelled out into the nothingness as she ran. She stumbled and scraped her hands and knees bloody against the hard floor.

She crawled then; she had to escape the nightmare. She had to wake up. To wake up and see Daniel again, to do things right, to tell him how she really felt. She crawled and crawled, scraping her fingers raw; she had to escape. An image like a movie started to appear, flashing before her eyes in the darkness, blinding her. She shielded her eyes with her bleeding arm. No, no, it was her life flashing before her eyes. She can't die; she had to wake from this nightmare. But maybe she should watch; maybe it would bring out an end. She opened her eyes. As they adjusted, she watched the images before her. A little girl with dark hair in a park playing alone as a small black fox watched with blood red eyes.

The little girl turned towards Mel, and Mel released a strangled gasp. The little girl was her. She was at a party at the park. She ran to the swings. Mel was confused. Was this a memory from her past? She didn't remember it. She gave up, sitting down and watching as the phantom of her youth played.

The other kids seemed to play amongst themselves as Mel swung on the rusty swing set. Her long hair flew around her as she watched the others, and then she gazed up at the clear blue sky. She jumped off at her highest height and flailed, landing on her hands and knees with a pout. Scrunching up her nose, she dusted herself off and ran to the table of burgers, grabbing two and a bag of chips.

Walking off with her plate, Mel sat next to a bush, munching on her chips. A small rustle in the dark green leaves next to her made her start. Looking side to side, she pushed the leaves of the bush apart to reveal a small black fox. Its eyes, an eerie crimson that sparkled in the afternoon light as the fox stared at the plate of food.

Mel split her burger, feeding the fox with a giggle as it ate from her hand. She shared her chips with the fox as well. Finished, she stood up, stretching toward the blue sky. As she walked away, a hand grabs her.

Turning, she came eye to eye with a boy who stood where the fox had been.

The boy had shaggy, ink-black hair and the same piercing red eyes. He seemed confused by his own actions as he let go. He ruffled her hair as he scrunched up his eyebrows. "I'd like to pay you back for the meal. What do you want?" he asked, sticking his hands into his pockets.

Mel turned her head to the side thinking. A grin grew on her face as she clapped her hands together. "Play with me!"

The boy stared incredulously at her but then nodded in agreement. The two played in the park. They ran around the plush green hills, climbed on the rusted colorful bars of the gymnasium, they watched the ducks that drifted lazily across the pond, and swung on the swings. The girl kept giggling with a large grin plastered across her face, while the boy had only a slight smirk.

Eventually, the sun started its descent and families began packing their things. Mel heard her mother call for her. The boy signaled her to follow him to the large trees that surrounded the park. She did as he requested, and found to her surprise, that the boy had grown into an older teen. She looked to where her mother was and took a step back.

"Don't be scared. I'm not going to hurt you. Come here," he said, beckoning her. She walked over slowly and he poked her forehead, pushing her backward. "This was fun, little brat, but this is goodbye. Some things are best forgotten." And with those words, everything went dark and disappeared into nothingness.

Chapter 35

Mel was confused, holding her head in her hands. "What's going on?" she questioned, rising and continuing her way, still in the darkness. Her feet hit stone as a muggy breeze ruffled her hair. The sound of something dripping and swishing echoed bouncing off the walls.

"What?" Mel touched the mossy stone wall that had seemed to appear next to her. She followed it down, seeing a light ahead as the swishing grew louder.

She stepped into the light and found a cave, its walls lined high with woven baskets. In the middle of the cave, on a large stone, sat a young man weaving a basket. Mel covered her mouth in shock when she saw his fluffy black tail and fox like ears atop his head that twitched ever so often. His messy black hair covered his face, yet he looked like the person from that memory.

"Hell-hello," Mel said, taking a cautious step forward.

He looked up at her, his red eyes glowing in the sparse light, an air of boredom radiated off him as he studied her disheveled appearance.

"Hey," was all he said as he went back to weaving the light brown basket.

Mel collapsed as her body shook violently. She threw her head back, laughing hysterically as the stranger watched with a raised eyebrow. "I'm sorry it's just, this has been the most horrid and craziest of dreams. Oh man, it's so messed up. I'll have to tell Daniel tomorrow. We might laugh about it later. Thank goodness," she said, wiping some tears from her eyes as she trembled.

"You can't and it's not," the stranger replied with a quick jerk of his tail.

"What? What do you mean? This is only a dream. A bad one, but still a dream. I'll wake up any moment!" Mel snapped. She was at her emotional limit at this point. She just wanted to wake up from this nightmare.

"It's not a dream, so forget about waking up. That kid's dead, taking the eternal dirt nap now. Dead. Gone," he said, making hand motions of pushing something away.

"How can you say something like that!?" she questioned, her throat starting to close up as tears began to well up again.

"After you live for a few lifetime's, things like death mean little," he replied, with a small nod.

Mel jerked up, attempting to slap him but her wrist was caught. She struggled weakly, stopping when he stared at her like a parent scolding a small child. He released her wrist, pushing her back. She stumbled, bringing her hands to her chest, clenching them. He had gone back to weaving, ignoring her.

Mel stared down at the dirty rock floor under her as the cave walls spun around her. Her head was dizzy and she felt sick. Her voice cracked as she threw back her head again but this time she released a wretched howl like that of a wounded animal. Her sobs bouncing off the cave walls made it sound like multiple people were suffering with her, but it was only her, wailing and dry heaving when she needed to breathe.

Back in the woods. Victor kept his insults going, but stopped when he noticed the girl had stopped reacting. He looked at her, noticing her blank eyes devoid of light. The steady rising of her chest signaled that she was alive but she looked like a lifeless doll. "Hey! Listen to me!" he yelled violently, jerking her head back and forth, but she didn't react, just continued to stare into the distance.

"What the hell! Wake up! It's no fun if you're not terrified and pleading for your life!" He slapped her so hard she slammed to the floor yet there was no reaction. He started kicking her and stomping on her. "It's no fun to kill a doll!"

He paused, hearing shouts. Cursing under his breath, he ran to the tree line. "Mel, I'll get you one day, but first I'll make you suffer till you beg for death. That's a promise," he said, sneering, before slinking into the wilderness.

Tsume was the first to enter the clearing. She scooped Mel up into her arms, ready to fight and defend her. "Who did this? Mel, what's wrong? It's me, Tsume." She cradled her and gave her a little shake, but Mel didn't react. She checked her pulse and released a sigh of relief.

"Tsume, is Mel hurt?" Johnathan asked, running to her side, his eyes darting around the area. A look of great sadness darkened his face.

"What's wrong? She's alive," Tsume asked, confused, lifting the bloodied girl in her arms.

Johnathan clenched his hands trembling and turned his head toward Kiba who held Daniel. Revelation flashed across her face as she shook her head. The other two just turned away.

Johnathan ripped the scythe from the ground, a scowl darkening his face. His fingers turned white as he clutched it. He glared at the weapon as if he blamed it for this tragedy.

"We need to take Mel to the infirmary," Johnathan said. His voice was thick and shaky, as he fought back tears.

"We should go after that monster! It was obviously Victor!" Tsume yelled.

"Don't be an idiot. There's nothing we can do now. He's escaped. Mel's health is top priority right now," Johnathan snapped before storming off toward the village.

Kiba and Tsume followed behind in silence, both carrying a heavy burden of sadness as the blood red sun rose, lighting their path.

A basket smacked onto Mel's head. She lifted it up to see the fox man before her, discomfort clear on his face. Her lip trembled as a fresh wave of tears started and he pushed the basket back down over her face.

"You know, you could thank me for saving your life, and stop crying," he said, pushing down on the basket.

"Thank you for what?" She sniffled, trying in vain to remove it from her head.

"Saving you. I ripped your consciousness away from your body, putting you in a coma like trance. It wasn't a hard thing to do with you in such a state like..." he paused to make hand gestures at her. "This. Anyway it kept that guy from killing you."

A light flickered in her head. She knew this voice! It was the voice from the snake attack, the one that stopped her from sulking in her room after the thieves. "Th...thank you for...for everything..what's your name?" she muttered as her silent tears fell. She pushed up the basket to look at him.

The look of surprise was evident on his face as his left ear twitched. "Drake," he replied, softly placing a finger to her fore-head. "My work here is done. You're safe now. Good night. It's time to wake up." he pushed her back.

Mel fell into darkness again, falling and falling. With a start, her eyes flew open, the white walls of the room blinded her for a moment. She rubbed her eyes with bandaged hands and looked around the infirmary.

Chapter 36

Mel turned her stiff neck to see her uncle and teacher sitting beside her bed. "Hey," she croaked out meekly.

Lupus smiled gently patting her head, a look of concern crossing his face as she shrunk away from the contact on reflex. "You went through a terrible experience, but you're safe now."

"Tell me it was a dream," she begged, her eyes pleading.

Johnathan turned away. "I'm sorry, I understand what you are going through, but you shouldn't have left the perimeter."

"You're sorry. You understand," Mel said darkly. A strange anger boiling up inside her.

"Mel, we need to talk about this scythe," Johnathan said, after giving her a worried look. He pulled out the black scythe, and placed it on the foot of her bed. The blade had retracted back to its compact, bow-like appearance.

"If you contracted the patron demon that owns it, you would technically be in line as second now," Lupus said, looking her in the eye.

"Second, as in second in command, as in Johnathan's job? That is what you are worried about?!" She paused, looking at her bandaged hands, releasing a strangled laugh. "What kind of sick joke is this? Daniel's dead, I was attacked, and this is what you talking to me about; this is what's important? I've done nothing but fail since the day that demon bear attacked me and you say I'm special now because of a scythe. Do I have to remind you that Daniel died?!"

Johnathan looked at her as his face changed to that of revelation in horror as he turned to look at Lupus. "That's what you did with the bear. How could you, she's your niece!"

"Johnathan, please calm down. It's not like that." Lupus said, holding his hands up.

"Now what!?" Mel croaked out.

"Johnathan. Don't," Lupus warned.

"Your uncle set you up from the very beginning. The demon that attacked you. Lord Lupus captured it and placed it there."

Mel didn't think anything else could shake her crumbling sanity, but that sentence was the tipping point. "I almost died...I almost died! My sister could have died...Alma could have died! How could you? This is all your fault! Why? Why?" she pleaded clenching her hands.

"Melosia, please calm down. Your injuries will open back up. I know Lord Lupus went too far this time but please calm down." Johnathan attempted to placate her, but she smacked his hand away, fully taken over by her rage and indignation.

"Oh, yeah I forgot," she sneered, her body feeling warm. She wanted to scream. She had been beaten, broken, and betrayed. "You're sorry. You understand. As if you could ever understand my pain!"

The smack echoed clear through the infirmary. Mel's head was turned to the side from the impact. Johnathan stared at his outstretched hand in shock and instant regret. Rage, shame, and sadness boiled up inside her, overflowing in that instant.

"GET OUT! GET OUT! GET OUT!" she screamed at the top of her lungs as the tears cascaded again. She kept screaming, crying, and began throwing the cups and plates that were on the nightstand, smashing them to pieces to chase them away. She kept screaming and crying, refusing to eat. She kept screaming and crying into the night until her voice was raw and ruined.

Mel sat in the room, staring at her trembling hands. A sinking feeling of despair, nausea, betrayal, and regret made her insides squirm painfully. Wrapping her arms around herself, she dug her fingers into them as the white walls of the infirmary closed in around her. The world was spinning off axis, crooked and wrong.

Fresh tears burned in the corners of her eyes while her dark hair fell around her like a curtain to hide her from the world. She was actually surprised she still had tears to cry, unlike her voice which she had screamed raw. At this point, her voice was hoarse and cracked, broken, just like she was, sitting there wallowing in misery.

What had gone wrong? What had she ever done to deserve this pain? How could her uncle betray her like this? Just when everything in her life finally felt like it was right like she had purpose it was snatched away with reality's icy grip. The happiness she had thought she found came crashing down like heavy rain, just like the day that her uncle had set up.

She wished that her uncle's plan had failed and the bear had just eaten her.

Reaching to the small wooden side table, the girl's fingers flicked over the cold metal of the butter knife. She gingerly lifted it up, twirling it in between her bandaged fingers, watching the reflection of candlelight flashing eerily in the blade. She let out a bitter laugh. She ran away from a boring life only for it to break into a thousand pieces of glass. What was the price of adventure and happiness?

Mel brought the knife up close to her face. In its shining blade, she could see her broken expression and the blotchy bruise from where Johnathan had struck her. She grit her teeth in annoyance, self-loathing, maybe anger, she didn't even know, as her long hair dripped over her face. Staring at herself she came to a hasty decision. She grabbed a fistful of her hair and violently hacked at it with the butter knife. Ragged chunks of hair pooled around the bed as she hacked and slashed, casting it to the side. With a heavy breath, she placed the knife back. Her neck felt colder and her head felt lighter. She gazed with some regret at the dark tendrils that lay coiled about like serpents.

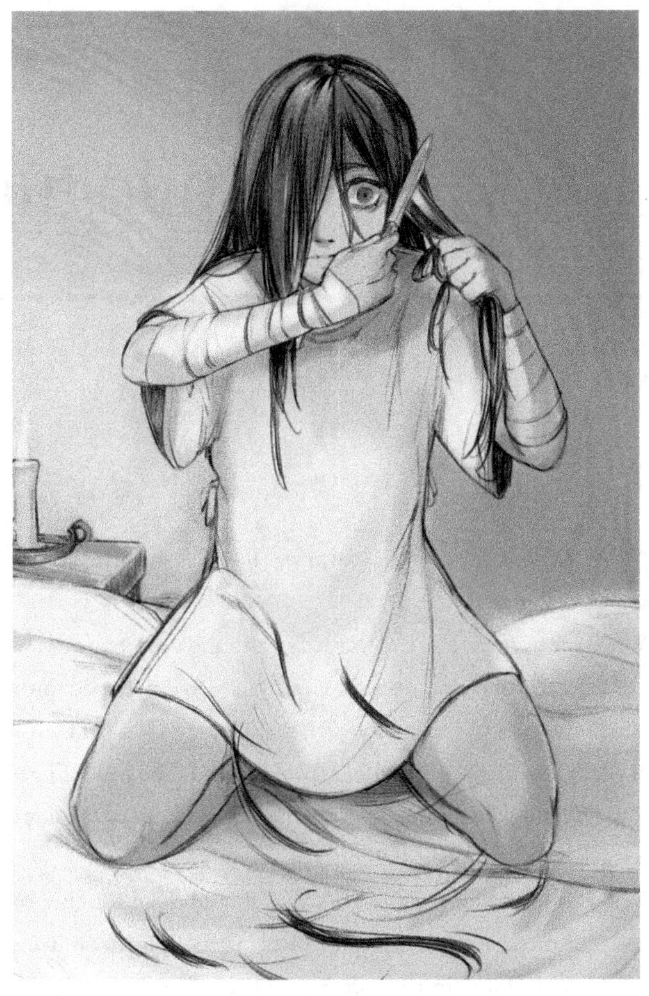

Epilogue

The scythe in its compact form was heavy as she lifted it up and carried it away.

When she hunted, Mel had learned stealth and used it now, walking out of the infirmary, making not a single sound as she slipped through the shadows. Without being spotted, she silently closed her bedroom door. A happy meow greeted her from the bed. She put a finger to her lips and shook her head, Savannah cocked her head to the side and nodded, leaping onto her shoulder.

Mel grabbed handfuls of clothes, and shoved them into her rucksack. She glanced at her nightstand, noticing the compact mirror, its gilded lilies gleaming in the soft candle light. Gently taking it into her hands, she stared at it, transfixed. Yet again, a wave of unwanted emotion crashed over her like a tsunami. Raising the mirror over her head, she brought her arm down in a swift arc, though only silence followed as her fingers refused to release the treasured object. Sinking down to her knees, she held the mirror to her chest, taking calming breaths.

Savannah rubbed against Mel's cheek, bringing her back. Mel scratched her behind the ear, asking in a whisper if she wanted to leave with her. The cat nodded, her golden eyes gleaming. With that, the two slipped out of the room to the kitchens and then out of the mansion.

Mel kept her head down, shielding her face with her choppy hair. The moon was high, covered by a thick layer of clouds. It was the dead of night. Not a soul could be seen. How many days had it been? She wondered, making her way to the white fence from a time that was almost a year ago. She walked through the head-stones until she found what she looked for. A grave that had been freshly made and that held something that was invaluable to her. She wiped roughly at the tears that burned in the corners of her eyes before kneeling and placing the mirror between the white flowers that already rested there.

"I don't know what you all believe in other than the spirits of nature, but I pray for your soul, Daniel. You were too good. You would try and stop me from what I'm going to do. But I can-can't stop. What do I even have to lose," Mel paused as her throat burned, and taking a deep breath, she continued. "I cared for you so much. Mi corazon. That's why on your grave, I swear I will make him pay. In blood, in pain, and in death, I will make him suffer. I'll have my vengeance for you, even if it kills me. Don't worry, you won't be lonely for long; after I avenge you, I'll probably join you."

After a moment of silence, she slipped into the stables. Her mare, Sandy, was tired but happy to see her. After giving her a treat, Mel went to work saddling her, tying a bow, a sword and the scythe to the saddle, and making sure the straps were tight. She pulled a traveling cloak from the wall and draped the old fabric over herself. Leading the horse through the gates, Mel gazed up at the dark cloudy sky as a crisp breeze ruffled her hair. She sniffed the air, knowing that the earthy smell meant rain. That was good, it would hide her trail. And what better way to take the next step; coming full circle. It was just like the day that started it all so long ago near the cabin in the woods with her family. A bitter smile curled upon her lips as she rose onto her horse, giving one last look at her home, pulling the cloak's hood up. Turning she spurred the mare forward, toward her destiny. If everyone was going to assume that she ran away from her problems, then run away she would.

Acknowledgements

Thank you to my friends and family for their support and encouragement.

Thank you Katy for the beautiful cover and art. Her handle is katy @_inktho on all socials if you'd like to check out her amazing work.

Lastly, Thank you for giving my love letter to anime and fantasy novels a read.

About the Author

Liz has a bachelors in Biology and a handful of different medical related certifications (a certified vampire being one of them). She is a fur mom to one clingy pitbull and has a full time job just to give her sweet boy the life he deserves. She was raised on pokemon and yugioh, the campy line delivery of the 4kids dubs lives in her soul. A lover of video games, books and anime, she wanted to write books for those who wish to be dropped into worlds of fantasy, whimsy, and horror. She is excited to share this new world with others and to add published author to her titles.

You can find her at lizzyhen on Tumblr.